S

The Great Mormon Cricket Fly-Fishing Festival and Other Western Stories

The Great Mormon Cricket Fly-Fishing Festival

and Other Western Stories

Tom Bishop

UNIVERSITY OF NEW MEXICO PRESS ❧ ALBUQUERQUE

©2007 by the University of New Mexico Press
All rights reserved. Published 2007
Printed in the United States of America

12 11 10 09 08 07   1 2 3 4 5 6 7

LIBRARY OF CONGRESS CATALOGING-IN-PUBLICATION DATA

Bishop, Tom, 1937–
    The great Mormon cricket fly-fishing festival and other
western stories / Tom Bishop.
            p. cm.
    ISBN-13: 978-0-8263-3928-7 (PBK. : ALK. PAPER)
1. Western stories.
2. West (U.S.)—Social life and customs—Fiction.
I. Title.
    PS3602.I766G74   2007
    813'.6—dc22
                            2006029417

Book and cover design and
    type composition by Kathleen Sparkes
This book is typeset using Janson 10/14, 23P6
    Display type is Latino Elongated

*This book is for my wife, Buellah,
whose patience, tolerance, and support
have been and are deeply appreciated.*

Contents

Preface

WHEN I WAS VERY YOUNG, I STOOD ON THE TALLEST ROCK AND SAW the country, and I knew I belonged there. I saw how the mountain reached out and gathered the land to itself to keep it from falling apart. I saw how the mountain held the sky above it. We all were one.

I heard stories of people who had been there before me, and I see people who are there today who have their own stories. There were and are so many stories of people in the country that I had to write some of them so as to not forget or tangle them.

Even though the West as a frontier ceased to exist after 1890, the West as an emotion or, in some cases, as a cultural and social experience lingered far into the twentieth century, and vestiges still are present in small places today. It is a part of the sense of history that humans carry and that we have such a strong tendency to nurture.

I was fortunate to not just meet but to live with men and women who in their vibrant youths had been a part of the real West. They all are gone now, those who remembered. In the bunkhouse at night some of them told their remembrances and recounted their adventures and experiences. I was just old enough to listen and to remember. Later, I witnessed and later some things happened to me.

The twentieth century West, at least where I was, barely could have been considered civilized until after World War II. That was when great changes came to my part of the West. I remember the first power hay stacker in the country, a Second World War truck. I remember the first tractor in the country, a small, red Farmall Cub. I certainly didn't get to use it. The boss used it; I still raked hay with a team of horses.

The twentieth century was an exciting time. The stories need to be told.

Tom Bishop
Atlantic City, Wyoming
June 2005

Acknowledgments

I am indebted to John Langan for his help with the Lakota language and to Irving Garbutt for his historical assistance. I also appreciate very much Philappina Halstead's remarkable patience and diligence in reading and finding my blunderings.

A Long Time Ago...

The Vision of Hehaka 'To

⤳

THE GRAY, CRYSTALLINE SKY SAT LIKE THICK ICE OVER A BEAVER DAM, closing out the rest of the world. Under the sky there were bleak, sloping ridges that the wind had swept clean, brushing the snow into the washes and valleys so that from above the land looked like a giant white tree that had fallen over the earth-colored ridges. In the valleys there only were the slender red, iron-topped points of old willows, although an occasional gray skeleton of a cottonwood reached up-ward. The air was rigid and made a man walk as though he were in a dream, unable to run.

Cetan hupahu moved slowly along one of the ridges that ran toward the big white mountain, Wica cepa hala, in the distance. He had been walking toward the mountain for three days.

He wore a hat of beaver, dark and shiny, and a buffalo-hide coat that was the color of the ridges, the fur inside for warmth, and under the coat he wore his buckskin shirt. His leggings were elk hide and moccasins buffalo hide, the fur on the inside. Buffalo mittens shielded his hands. On his back under his coat he carried snowshoes and his ash bow strung with buffalo sinew inside its buckskin case with the quiver attached, the quiver full of arrows. At his side he also carried a metal-bladed knife that had come from the Wasicu, and a Wasicu axe with a metal head, its handle wrapped in red Wasicu blanket. Only his eyes, black as onyx, did the cold touch, so nestled was he in the fur of his wraps. Even his large nose and high cheekbones were safe from the ice crystals that hung like one continuous curtain in the air.

It was as cold as two winters before when Igmu Matowin had become sick and weak from the long winter, and their small daughter Tzing Cikala had died. Then his lodge had been filled with sadness as if a great rock had settled on it. The lodge seemed empty and forgotten. The only life he could remember from that time was the low keening of Igmu Matowin for the loss of their small daughter, who had not lived long enough to know how good the earth was or to gather its white and blue and red and yellow flowers that held the rays of Onaste in their blooms.

He was as cold as he ever had felt, in this ice-world that hovered over him like an eagle over the stone mountains, suspended. It was so cold that he could smell nothing but the startling and terrifying ice in the air.

That morning, when he had left his shelter among the rocks, he had asked of the elk, "Hehaka, nitawoyuha kin ota ehantana, kaotalaks'e wicako wo," because he and the people who were left of the *tiospaye* needed very badly that which their brother the elk had to give.

This winter they would have had plenty to eat if the Skidi hadn't come late in the fall. They had struck suddenly and quickly. Igmu Matowin and their new son, Ista samna cikala, and other women and children and old ones had found shelter in the fall-shredded willows, where they had been protected by armed men, so that the Skidi were afraid to come into the heavy brush after them. But the Skidi had taken all of their buffalo and deer and elk and antelope, and most of their horses. Many of their lodges and other belongings also had been destroyed before they could drive the Skidi away.

Cetan hupahu had stepped from the willows and driven his lance through a Skidi who had ridden his swift, cream colored warhorse too close the willows. The Skidi had been covered with red paint except for the lower part of his face, which had been painted black, and the brown hands painted on his chest to show he had killed an enemy. Killing the Skidi had made Cetan hupahu feel good knowing that his enemy would never kill again, especially any of the Lakotah. Cetan hupahu had kept the Skidi's short, black scalp, but when he saw the tiospaye after the Skidi had destroyed it, he knew he would have to hunt again. All the people of the tiospaye had known then that they would have to hunt before Waziyata gathered up his mantle of snow to let things grow again.

They had only taken the time to see that the dead women and children and old ones were placed in cottonwoods so that their spirits might leave them freely. Then, with whatever they could find, they had left the valley to find relatives to live with for the winter.

In the new tiospaye, they lived with his cousin, Mato Topa, who had given willingly of his things, shared with them so that they might live. Now he had seen a new flush of life come to Igmu Matowin. She had feared as much as he that perhaps they might lose the new one, the son, who seemed to be strong, who might have starved if Mato Topa had not brought them to his lodge to share with them.

Mato Topa's tipi was crowded, but he had made room, and Igmu Matowin had joined in helping to make everyone as comfortable as possible. Cetan hupahu's heart had been filled with the warmth in Mato Topa's lodge, and he had promised himself to make a good hunt for the people of the new tiospaye as soon as he could.

When the time came for him to hunt, he had taken a sweat bath with his cousin and the *wicasa wakan*, Mato Wankaguya. There with the wicasa wakan and his cousin, the Great Spirit had come to him and shown him many blue elk in front of a white hill.

When he told the wisaca wakan and his cousin what he had seen, Mato Wankaguya, who was old and whose skin hung in limp pleats from his skinny arms, had said, "Waste, Cetan hupahu."

So there also he had prayed—"Hehaka, nitawoyuha kin ota ehantana, kaotalakes'e wicaku wo"—because he had seen a great herd of blue elk running and running and running, so many that he could not begin to count them all, running toward him through the snow, as many as he could see in a day.

Igmu Matowin had taken his buckskin hunting shirt and had sewn a blue elk of porcupine quills on it to help him find the elk he had seen. The elk were sewn next to the dried hawk's wing on his shirt to give them more strength, and he had felt good in his heart at seeing what his wife had done for him and for the people.

He had done everything he could to assure himself of the blessing of the Great Mystery, Wakan Tanka. Although the hunt was for the people who were in need of their brother the elk, Cetan hupahu did not know whether the Great Mystery would answer his prayer.

When he was a child in his father's lodge, the lodge of Sunka hanble, he had heard his father tell of a time long ago when men came into camp and told everyone that the hunters should get ready for the great elk herd to come because they had seen in the distance a dark line with haze like a dust storm over it: the elk running before the winter that was coming. The older, experienced men of the camp had gone to the hills to watch for enemies, and the young hunters had gathered their bows and arrows and knives, and the horse herd was driven into the camp for the hunters.

In a narrow place in the sharp hills, the hunters waited in two lines facing each other, each hunter with an arrow ready to shoot, another held tightly in his mouth, and more in his quiver. The earth began to rumble beneath their feet, and then the elk came, first the great bulls, the dark necks bulging, their antlers swaying, their red tongues lolling. They were bellowing, all of them together, like thunder across the plains. They came through the narrow opening between the high hills, the bulls, the cows and the calves, more than anyone had ever seen together at once, like a brown blanket thrown over the earth by the Great Mystery. The pass was full of the roar of the elk, and the hunters began to shoot, and elk fell, but on they came as leaves in the fall blown along the ground.

Near the end, stragglers among the elk tried to retreat from the smell of blood, but wolves behind them made them turn around again and rush the narrow gap. Still the hunters killed them, until the ground no longer shook with their hooves, and the elk herd passed from sight.

The people had butchered fallen elk until long after dark, and every lodge had enough meat to last through the winter.

Cetan hupahu was remembering that story that night when he scooped a place in the snow to build a small fire in the shelter of a rocky draw, and while he chewed pemmican. And then he remembered how Igmu Matowin had looked to him the first time he had seen her. He thought of her soft, smooth skin and her large, black eyes and long hair, and how she had walked in front of him as he sat with his cousin, and how they looked at each other and smiled and shook their heads knowingly, as if they knew everything there was to know in the whole world, everything they owed to Wakan Tanka.

It had happened after he and his cousin came back from taking horses from the Susuni beyond the stream called the Popo Agie by the Susuni. He had taken three horses and a scalp. She walked in front of him wearing a rich dress of light buckskin with porcupine-quill workings she had done, to show that she was good with her hands. Her face was red with berries, and her hair was combed smooth so that it glistened in the sunlight.

She walked away from camp into the willows along the stream, and he followed to accidentally bump into her. She did not even look at him, but walked past him as if he didn't exist.

He spent a year with his cousin in his tiospaye courting her. He went to Mato Wankaguya, and for a good, rich buffalo robe he had traded a flute made from the two halves of a cedar stick glued together and bound with sinew. It had five finger holes and an air vent that could be closed with a movable piece of wood. It was carved in the shape of a horse's head, and Mato Wankaguya told him, "The Great Spirit has touched this flute, Cetan hupahu, and I will give you a song I have made that no young woman will be able to resist. But you must play and sing just as I tell you, or nothing will happen."

"I will do as you tell me," he said.

He also made up a song of his own, and sometimes he sang, "My love, come to me in the night, and we will be together."

He spent many nights that summer in the brush near her father's tipi, playing his magic flute and singing the magic song given to him by Mato Wankaguya. He would come and stand in front of the lodge and talk to her. Sitting at his small fire in the snowy gully, he smiled to think of the things he had talked about when he came to her that way.

"There is a gooseberry bush beyond the bend that will have enough berries this fall to fill several baskets. I found it today when I walked that way," he would say.

"I know where the bush is," she would say.

"My cousin and I are going with some friends to steal horses from the Susuni," he would say.

"Your cousin is a good man," she would say.

They talked of everything but what they wanted to talk about. Then, later, he came to her father's tipi and threw his robe over her and himself and, in front of anyone interested enough to watch them, he embraced her, and they talked about other silly things.

Finally, he said, "I have many horses from the Skidi. How many should I bring to tie outside your father's tipi?"

"Five," she smiled.

He brought five good horses, two bays, two red ones, and a small stallion taken from the Susuni the year before, the horse with the spots on its rump that had come from another people beyond even the Susuni.

All this he remembered as he looked into his small fire in the cold night. From a long buckskin bag with blue and white beadwork, he took a small pipe made from a hollow deer bone and packed it with tobacco from the bag. While he smoked, he remembered the winter two years ago when there was no food in the tiospaye and their first small one had died, Igmu Matowin had looked like a loose buckskin bag. He had thought that neither of them would ever smile again. Their small daughter had wasted away until she did not even have tears or sobs left in her little body. Finally, she did not have any breath left, either.

Only when their son Ista samna cikala came did Igmu Matowin smile again.

Then, when the Skidi raided their tiospaye she stopped smiling again. Ista samna cikala had not made any sound, either, until they came to his cousin's lodge. And even then, Igmu Matowin had not smiled freely. There was a difference between the way she smiled when she was happy and the way she smiled when she was trying to look happy.

Before dawn came, Cetan hupahu said to his brother the elk, "Hehaka, nitawoyuha kin ota ehantana, kaotalakes'e wicacu wo," and then he was walking again. When day came he always walked upward toward the white, pointed Wica cepa hala, walking steadily along the top of a ridge where there was no snow but only the gray, icy sky.

As long as he walked, he did not see or hear any birds, not even ravens, nor did he see any tracks other than a few tiny rabbit tracks, haphazard and halting in the small valleys where lonesome willow branches marked the course of a frozen stream buried in snow. He had not even seen a hawk hunting the rabbit. His walking was tortured with slowness, as though the cold was barring his way.

Once he stopped and hunkered on a ridge and chewed a piece of pemmican, letting it thaw in his mouth, tasting the jerky and berries and fat that made saliva run in his mouth. While he rested, he thought of the Great Mystery and of his vision, and he wondered whether he would be allowed to find the elk he had seen so clearly, the blue elk. The Great Mystery heard all prayers, but who could tell if a prayer would be answered?

Cetan hupahu knew he had to go toward the three-pointed white mountain, Wica cepa hala. Once there, either something would happen or nothing would happen, whatever the Great Mystery chose for him. He reached inside his buffalo coat and touched his hawk charm and then ran his fingers over the blue elk that Igmu Matowin had sewn so carefully for him. Doing that gave him a strong heart, and he stood and began again to follow the ridge toward the white mountain that continually grew larger.

The sky was so hazy with ice crystals that seldom did he actually see the sun as it traveled across the sky. He saw it as only a brighter hazy thing in the gray sky, and for a while he kept pace with it, but finally it began to outdistance him, and then he could see the dark line above the white plains that marked the start of the pine hills that eventually led to the white mountain. When he thought of entering the hills where the snow would be deep, he feared that he would not find the blue elk. Certainly they would not go into the deep snow.

When the sun sank, the sky became a faded orange like a fire dying away and then black, but he still walked, not wanting to take the time to rest. He followed the ridge in the dark.

Suddenly, he became aware of dark shapes near him, and then more dark shapes around him, and finally he came close to one and saw that it was a wolf. The wolf ignored him, so he kept walking. Then there were other shapes in the night, and he could finally smell them, so many of them that their musky odor filled his nostrils, the first thing he had been able to smell in four days of walking.

He dared not think of them. He did not know whether to think of them, right then, would be good or bad, so he did nothing, and finally he came to a stand of pines on the side of the ridge above the valley, and he sat down and leaned back against one of them. All night he listened to the wolves. Sometimes one of the large, dark shapes came near where he sat, awake and waiting for the day to come.

When the black at last faded and the sky was deep pink and dark blue, he saw more elk than he had ever seen before, more than one person could count in a day. The great herd was black, as though night had not left the white valley at the foot of the pine hills. As the day became stronger the breath of the herd formed a blue cloud over the valley, and the elk themselves seemed blue because of the light seeping through the cloud.

Cetan hupahu eased his mittens from his hands and let his coat slip from his shoulders. Carefully he took his bow and quiver from his back, the bowstring warm and flexible from being next to his body under the coat. He fitted an arrow, and when he let it go, the arrow struck a nearby cow right behind her shoulder. She floundered into a drift of snow, and instantly, he was upon her, slitting her throat and feeling her warm blood run over his hands. Then he said a prayer: "Aho, hehaka, kola waste! Pila Miya, Wakan Tanka, Aho, pila miya, Tunkasila Wakan. Wakan Tanka wopila k'upi kin he waste!"

When he looked up, the great herd was moving all at the same time and wolves were taking stragglers, the old ones and the calves. The great herd moved down the valley and across the ridges, a brown blanket thrown over the white snow. Using his knife and axe, he bled the elk and butchered her, and from her ribs he made a sled tied with her sinew. He skinned her and packed the fresh meat in the skin and tied the bundle with more sinew. When he had his snow-shoes on, he pulled his sled of meat with a thong of her hide, walking quickly, following a great blue cloud down the valley through snow that had been trampled hard enough to walk upon easily.

All day Cetan hupahu traveled down the valley, walking easily on the trampled snow. Along the trail there were wolves, some sitting or lying next to white bones in the red snow, already sated, resting before taking the trail of the herd again, others trotting down the valley after the elk that he, too, followed, pulling his rib sled behind.

Even with his fur wraps tight about his face, he felt the terrible cold and he did not try to run, because that would make him breathe harder and pull even more of the cold into his chest. He walked faster where the valley was flatter, but he always took care not to tire himself too much.

When he came to Pankeska Wahpa, he crossed on the thick ice, still in the trail of the great elk herd, and when late in the day he turned and looked back, he saw three wolves coming along his trail, a large gray one with his tail in the air, the other two coming in single file behind the leader. Before darkness came, he looked back again. The large one was still coming behind him, but the other two had swung wide and paralleled him, one on each flank.

The sled was very heavy, and moving uphill in the deepest snow he could find so he could walk with his snowshoes and pull his sled, he had to go slowly. His eyes burned, both from the snow and from lack of sleep the night before. When night came, he continued to follow the great elk trail. Even without moonlight it was easy to follow. The great trail was wide and edged with the carcasses of the weak that had been taken by the wolves, dark patches of fur on the white snow, and all around him he could hear the wolves.

He finally stopped in the middle of the trail, his legs tight with weariness, his chest heaving, and his eyes hot. He stepped back to his sled and watched the blackness for the wolves, but nothing seemed to move. He took off his heavy coat and slipped off his bow case and quiver, then put his coat back on. He sat down next to the sled and the meat bundle and rested against the elk's fur.

From twigs he had taken in the small valley and dried grass he had carried with him from the first day, he carefully built a fire, chipping a flint spark into the grass and blowing softly until it flared. He added the twigs and then small pieces of aspen, until the little fire began to warm his hands. He let a piece of pemmican thaw in his mouth, and then he chewed quietly, savoring the taste.

Beyond the tiny fire Cetan hupahu saw the yellow eyes of a wolf and then the outline of the wolf lying in the white snow. He listened for the others, but he heard nothing. After the fire went out, he waited a long time for the wolf to come close, but it didn't move, and finally he closed his eyes.

For a long time Igmu Matowin had not smiled after she had found that she carried another child in her. It seemed to him that he could always see behind her face the fear that something new would happen to take this child, too. They had not talked much during the winter, because both of them remembered how the other small one had died. But he could see that she cared very much for the child she was carrying. She took good care of him and herself through the winter, and she grew heavier all the time, but her beautiful smile she did not show him.

Finally, the time of Waziyata passed, and Waziyata picked up his white blanket, and the earth woke from its sleep and the grass greened and breezes became warm and flowers came to flow like many-colored paints down the draws, and when Tinpsinla itkahca wi came, so did the new son of Cetan hupahu and Igmu Matowin, and Igmu Matowin finally smiled again.

Cetan hupahu took his new son into the warmth of Tinpsinla itkahca wi and held him to the Great Spirit and said, "Cinksa, mahpiya no maka na taku el hiyeye kin oyas'in ablega ye." From then until the time when the Skidi came, they had been truly happy again.

It was tugging that woke him. One moment he was asleep, and the next he was facing the wolf. "Yaaa!" he yelled, and the wolf retreated a few feet, where it again took up its waiting position on the snow. It lay looking at him, shifting its eyes away from him, unable to hold the man's eyes, its tongue lolling out its mouth. Cetan hupahu searched the darkness for the other two wolves and found them hunkered in the snow, one to each side of him, farther back than the leader.

Cetan hupahu breathed carefully, and taking his knife, he cut a sinew that bound the meat. With his axe he cut three pieces of the frozen meat away from the bundle, and saying, "O Sunkamanitu, taku sice kin etanhan sunglakupi ye," he tossed each wolf a piece of frozen meat.

He did not sleep the rest of the night. When just the first of the dawn showed against the distant horizon, he stood and raised his arms and said, "Wakan Tanka. Noge can oyaglukse lapa? He wapanlulah cake c'un! Etulake kin waku'kte. Wican'an wan econ mayasi kin he owotanlu edamon hunse'? O Mita Kuye Oyasin."

Then, grasping the leather thong, he once again set out, keeping to where the wind had blown the snow to make his journey as easy as possible. He followed the great herd, and behind him came the three wolves, trotting, their red tongues hanging loosely in their mouths.

In the afternoon, he saw three horsemen on a ridge. They sat on their horses, two of them each leading a horse. They were watching him. Cetan hupahu stopped and looked at them. If they were enemies, he could not hide. He was standing in the middle of a stream course where there were only sparse willows with their fingertips reaching out of the snow. Finally, the three horsemen turned and rode up the ridge toward him. He was so tired, he felt as though he were in a dream, floating along the top of the snow. When he turned to look for the wolves, they were not there. It was as if they had not ever really been there, not even their spirits.

When the horsemen came close, he saw his cousin and waved to him, and his cousin inched his horse down the slope toward the streambed.

When they met, Cetan hupahu said, "Hau, Kola."

"Hau, Kola, waste, Cetan hupahu. The wicasa wakan saw you coming with a burden. We came to find you."

"I have elk."

"We all have elk. You drove the elk to us. We have all the meat we need now. They came to us under a blue cloud, and we knew you had sent them to us," said Mato Topa.

From that day until the day he died, he called himself Hehaka 'To, and the Wasicu called him Blue Elk. His people knew why, and they spoke of him as Hehaka 'To and remembered him as the man who drove the elk. Afterward, every morning he said this prayer:

Wakan Tanka, wakan,
Let today be a day
Rich in good works,
A day of generosity
To all I meet.
All are my relations.
　　O Mita Kuye Oyasin

A Hundred Years Later...

Courting Miss Ellen

THE SLATE, SUNLESS SKY FINALLY HAD POURED ENOUGH GRAY INTO the store so that its corners had filled to the ceiling with odorless, charcoal shadows. Rain on the tin roof sounded like pebbles dropped into a bucket.

"Well?" Bob asked, standing behind the long counter, barren but for the silver register, a place to display but not to fondle hardware unattended, his hands on his hips making him look like a monstrous ewer, his back straight as though it were composed of a religious tenet rather than merely conventional bone. He exuded the suppleness of a stone pillar, but his beryl blue eyes glinted like polished stone.

The store smelled like ginger cookies and August fields, a scent moistureless and intimate. On the shelves arrayed in military line around the room were substantial rectangular and circular tins, and immaculate stacks of shirts, overalls, and rolls of materials, while against the back wall were staved barrels like soldiers. The huge, black stove had long since sucked the cold inside its belly and devoured it.

Hank lifted the burlap bag from the ash-colored wooden floor to the counter with arms that might have passed for dried willow limbs and said, "Stiff as frozen toes." He had carried the bag through molasseslike mud from the icehouse behind the store where he and Bob had put it the day before, next to a block of ice in the sawdust that was as cool as morning pasture grass on bare feet. When he spoke his voice was like a breeze in the pines.

Hank untwisted the rusted baling wire from the neck of the bag and let the neck flop to the counter. He pulled back the loose raveling of the bag until those standing at the counter could see a rattlesnake.

"See?" he said, looking up at Bob. With his brown eyes he appeared to be always on the verge of wanting to ask a question but not sure he should, as though the asking in itself might be a burden to someone. He appeared to live under an acute uncertainty.

"Pick it up," Bob said.

Hank, with his thumb and index finger, both of which looked like tiny, barkless pine sticks, picked up the rattlesnake behind its dry, greenish and bloated poison glands. "See?"

"My God, almighty," Tom said.

"Oh, hell, Tom, stand away if ya' think you'll git yer pretty face hurt," Sean said.

"Why, you're all crazy," Tom said, taking a step backward. "You'll git killed messin' with those things."

"Loosen up, Tom. We know what we're doing," Bob said. "Open its mouth, Sean."

"Well, I'm gittin'," Tom said.

"Then git," Sean said. His expression looked like that of a man ready to wrestle an opponent. He smelled dank, somber, and metallic like rocks. With a well-considered motion he inserted the head of the screwdriver between the snake's pliable jaws and mathematically turned it.

Bob took a pair of pliers from his pant pocket and extracted the snake's two fangs. "Drop him and let's do the next 'un," he said.

"Let's do 'em fast before they thaw out," Sean said, as though his idea had been a sudden inspiration, divinely guided.

"Relax. They ain't gonna do nuthin'," Bob said.

"Not these here, anyway," Hank added. He lay the rattlesnake on the floor at his feet, tenderly and indulgently. Then he touched the bottom of the sack as though it were a dry flower and gently gave it small, caressing tugs until another rattlesnake rolled out of the bag onto the counter. There were six of them.

The three remaining men watched the rattlesnakes as one by one they slowly and miraculously seemed to have been called back from death and given new flesh. They began to move, their tongues leaping like small, dark flames, their cherty eyes gathering an intenseness about them.

"Damn, they're beauties," Hank said.

"Nice ones," Bob said.

"Still spooks me," Sean said.

"Ya know they're harmless," Bob said.

"Today, maybe," Sean said.

"Good as dogs, and a lot cleaner," Hank said.

When the door opened, all three men looked up. The woman standing in the doorway had a body that resembled the porch pillars, and the expression of her face looked as though she were bent upon some indefinite and remote retribution. When she spoke her voice was like a dry twig being snapped. "More watchdogs, I see, Mister Jesper. Well, you can wait on me out here on the porch." She closed the door.

"Right away, Miss Ellen," Bob said, stepping respectfully over the rattlesnakes as he came around the end of the counter. "Excuse me, little fellers, but Miss Ellen is waiting for me." The wooden floor complained under the burden of his walking.

When he stepped out onto the porch, Miss Ellen was waiting for him, looking at him from under her bonnet through pearl eyes as though she had seen an injustice that nothing in this world possibly could rectify.

His eyes had taken on the aspect of an innocent child, even though his face was scored like a red, plowed field. "They're harmless; you know that, Miss Ellen."

"I detest them; you know that, Mister Jesper, and I will not enter your store as long as they are in there," she said.

"Yes, I know," he answered.

"I don't know why you can't have a watchdog like other people," Miss Ellen told him.

"Thieves ain't much afraid of watchdogs, and, anyways, ya cain't trust 'em; there as like as not to kiss a thief as bite 'em." He ran his hand through his curly, silver-lode hair and looked past Miss Ellen as though there were something about the bleak day that deserved his momentary study.

"Do not patronize me, Mister Jesper. I want a half pound of coffee, a pound of flour, and a tin of tomatoes," Miss Ellen said.

"Certainly, Miss Ellen," he said. His voice was like that of an actor speaking a fragile denouement, and when he touched her shoulder, he did it as though she were verbena.

When he came back inside, he saw that three of the rattlesnakes finally had moved away from the counter. "They're gittin' warm, ain't they," he said, as though he were alone on a stage rehearsing a line. When he carried Miss Ellen's goods to her, they stood together on the porch and watched a wagon and team of bay horses precariously settled at the top of the hill, awaiting some sort of sign to make them move. Finally he said, "Burial wagon."

"Such a dreary day, too, poor souls," Miss Ellen said.

When he went back inside he said, "Burial wagon comin'."

"Hell of a day fer a burial," Hank said.

The three men walked to the front window and watched, idly and speculatively, like children watching a parade form. A black and white spotted dog was lying on the pine coffin, its head resting in its crossed paws. The wagon came slowly down the hill, the driver with two women sitting next to him holding on to the brake to keep the wagon from slipping in the mud. Behind the first wagon was another, this one topped with a shaggy piece of gray canvas, the driver the only person who was not dressed in black other than the two small children sitting with him. Two men rode horses beside the wagon with the coffin as though they were guards for a precious cargo. Bob turned away from Sean and Hank and said, "I'll git dressed."

When he came back he was wearing a black coat that was shiny from disuse and bore with it the stringent odor of almost ceaseless storage.

"Diggin'll be easy," Sean said.

"Messy, though," Hank answered.

Bob opened the door and walked to the edge of the porch when the coffin wagon stopped in the street. The odor from the coffin was impatient and penetrating.

"I'm Robert Jesper," Bob announced to the mourners. They all looked the same, all to have been afflicted with the same disease as mourners always are, one that finally desensitizes any appetite other than an acute self-pity, a sameness holding in common the pathos of their species' desire to and inability to affect an unconquerable out-come. They had not yet become weary of retaliation against an impossibility. Their eyes glowed with unacceptance and ignorance of what the disaster meant. Only the dog looked like it knew the utter finality. "I'm the justice of the peace and the undertaker hereabouts 'cause I got the icehouse out back," he said with a flatness as though he were in another room.

"I'm the Reverend Jeremiah Hamm, and we have come from below Three Cripples to bury this unfortunate wife and mother, who belonged to this gentleman," he said, gesturing at one of the riders, as if he were flicking something noxious from his fingers, his voice quar-reling with his throat. "Perhaps we could have a small service for the deceased in your store out of the rain and store her in your icehouse until better weather?"

"Not in my store, Reverend. Never git the stink out, and she oughta be put under now, if ya don't mind me tellin' ya so," Bob answered.

"Fair enough, Friend. It's been a long haul since this morning when I come acrost these poor folks," the Reverend said. "Maybe a final farewell to the beloved on yer porch, Sir? Then we'll do our duty to her and cover her up."

"Good," Bob said. He turned his head and motioned to Sean and Hank whose faces, like children watching a Christmas tree, could be seen in the window. "Allow me to help ya, Ma'am," Bob said, reaching out to take an older woman's hand. She looked like she had been confused over a half-heard question.

"Yes, thank you," she said. "I'm the poor girl's mother-in-law, and Millie's the poor girl's sister-in-law," she said. Her voice was taut like a piece of wire. "We've had her like this for three days of mud. I wondered if there was anyplace where we could have a Christian burial. The Reverend's been a real help to us. I thought we'd have to leave her along the road. Road, did I say? Cow trail is more like it. Where in God's name are we?"

"Esterbrook, Ma'am," Bob answered. "Go get the sawhorses," he said to Sean and Hank.

One of the riders stepped onto the porch. The dog jumped off the coffin and followed the man. "Mud slowed us a couple a days," he said. He had the sensitive face of a messianic, and the sound of his voice was like nectar.

"Been rainin' off 'n' on fer three days, now," Bob said.

"Good thing we found this heah preacha'. He knew wheah ta' bring us. We kin bary her in peace now. Lahke a true Christian. We were on 'er way ta Jackson's Hole," he said, talking but looking away as though it was very important to say something and at the same time try to see a familiar face in an audience.

"Jackson's Hole's a long way off, yet," Bob said.

"Ta homestead," the young man said.

"Bad winters there," Bob answered him.

"Don't know what Ah'll do now."

"Trust in the Lord, Mister Smith," the Reverend said.

Hank and Sean came back with two sawhorses. They set them

on the porch, and Bob stepped back, using his hands the way an artist does to frame a painting and form a perspective, he motioned Sean to move one of the sawhorses.

"Yer porch is sloped," the Reverend said.

"Certainly it is; best to run water off," Bob answered. He motioned and Sean moved the sawhorse again, as though both his and Bob's concepts of the pathway to eternity lay between certain parallel planes from which there could be no deviation at all.

"No matter; it'll do," the Reverend said.

When the sawhorses were set with architectural precision, Bob looked up. Standing on the porch watching him as though his movements were part of a ceremonial form that had to be done to assure a proper and solemn perfection, were the old woman, the young Mr. Smith, and the others—the second rider, a pistol conspicuous under his black coat; the children, bewildered yet by the decisiveness of the event; and the hired driver, modestly attentive to the ritual of death. "All of ya go on 'n' step inside where it's warm and cozy. Me 'n' my men'll have this here set in a second," he said, motioning them toward the doorway. "Done it a million times."

When just he and the Reverend and Sean and Hank were left on the porch, he said, "All right, boys, set her on the sawhorses and let's git this done and quick. Goddamn, she stinks. Sorry, Reverend."

"No matter, Mister Jesper. She stinks," the Reverend replied.

Sean and Hank stepped off the porch into the mud, their footfalls in the mud making a muted sound like a failing pump. Hank climbed into the wagon, took a deep breath, and bent to move the coffin as Sean slid the other end across the wagon bed.

"All right," Bob said. He and the Reverend each took an end of the coffin as Hank and Sean lifted it, and they carried it to the sawhorses and lay it on them. "Let's git this done, Reverend, and git 'er in the ground."

"I'll make it short as I can with respect, Mister Jesper," he said.

"I shore as hell hope so," Hank said. "My God, why in hell couldn't they have buried her back there?"

"They're Christians, Sir," the Reverend said. "They had the children to think of, you know. Wanted the best for the poor children's mother, you know."

"Let's stop gabbin' and git 'er," Bob said. He looked across the street and saw Ellen and Mizzus Buell and Mizzus Carter standing together, sympathetic with the mourners, joining them in a tacit communion of the perplexity of an ultimate goal for which there only is anticipation without provision.

The moment Bob heard the man yell, "My God, I've been bitten by a rattlesnake!" he remembered them. "Oh my God," he said, and he looked at the door with the startled eyes of a man suddenly confronted by more than one imagined catastrophe.

The door erupted open and the second rider stepped out with his pistol in his hand. Shouting "Look out, ever'body; the place is full of 'em," he fired into the store.

"My God, don't shoot in the store!" Bob yelled and stepped forward to grab the man's arm. The younger woman appeared in the doorway, her eyes astonishingly open and porcelain, her mouth agape and unable to speak.

The man turned and hit Bob across his face with the pistol, and Bob fell backward into the coffin, knocking it off the sawhorses. The coffin crashed on the porch, its lid falling away and a corpse of what probably had been a young woman hung half in the coffin, the other half lying stiff off the porch in the mud, its face bloated and its colorless eyes and mouth terrifyingly open, as though she had been suddenly stunned by something outrageous.

The man fired again into the store, out of which ran the children, and the confused dog, barking raucously. As the old woman shoved the younger one in front of her, and both stumbled into the man with the pistol, she agitatedly asked everyone, "What have you done with my son's wife?" The husband now stood in the doorway, his lethargy finally dissipated, repeating metronomically, "I've been bit by a rattlesnake. I've been bit by a rattlesnake." Bob stood up and wiped his hand over his face. He could taste the tinny, red blood.

"Why, how, in God's name, did so many rattlesnakes get into your store, Mister Jespers?" the Reverend asked him. "I haven't ever seen so many in a store before. Minions of the Devil, Sir, at a Christian service."

Bob heard him, but he didn't answer. He stepped off the porch into the mud and walked across the road. He stopped walking when he reached the grass, where he bent and put his hands on his knees and let the blood drip from his broken nose.

He could hear the husband saying over and over, "I've been bit by a rattlesnake," the insipid sound of his voice a substanceless echo. A bolder voice was saying to him, "You crazy son-of-a-bitch," and Bob recognized the voice as the dead woman's brother. The Reverend was saying, "Now, now; think of the poor deceased," and her mother-in-law was repeating, "Will someone do something?" and always the sound of the panic-stricken dog punctuated their sentences, all of it sounding like discordant trumpets.

"Take my handkerchief," Miss Ellen said.

Bob saw her handkerchief. "Thank you," he said.

"You are quite welcome, Mister Jespers," she said. She touched his shoulder, delicately, as though he possessed a frailty.

I Cain't Go

I CAIN'T GO. I CAIN'T NEVER GO AGIN. AFTER ALL OF US MAKIN' ourselves look like a bunch of idiots like thet, I don't even see how they can even consider goin' out in public agin, much less goin' to a dance, where ever'body'll be starin' at us like we was a bunch of idiots, and didn't have no sense atall. I cain't believe we all went out there like thet lookin' fer them injuns like thet, 'n 'specially after Uncle Arnie told me 'n' William Hopkins we wasn't nuthin' but a couple of idiots fer even thinkin' 'bout doin' thet.

Well, we was warned. Next time someone comes along with a silly, fool idea like thet, I'm shore goin' to listen when Uncle Arnie says it's a silly, fool thing to do. If things hadn't been so borin' 'round here, I wouldn't a done it, you kin bet on thet. Jist like the day William Hopkins come ridin' in here all het up 'bout chasin' them injuns, all there was fer me to do was fiddle with thet bronc all day in the corral, but a man's gotta make his way somehow, 'n' once I thought bein' a top notch horsebreaker was jist the thing a man oughta do to make his way in this world, but thet was 'fore I found out 'bout horse breakin'.

Thet bronc, he was thet two-year-old bay thet Matilda foaled, 'n' I knew from the start he was goin' to be a humdinger. Jist two years old 'n' he'd look at ya like a dyed-in-the-wool spinster born with her mind already made up to say "No" and planned to go to the grave with a pleased conscience knowin' she had done said "No" all her life.

I done had thet two-year-old cornered in the corral and put my loop over his head jist as neat 'n' light as a snowflake, and when he started runnin', I dallied on the snubbin post, 'n' he hit the end of thet rope hard 'nough to jerk a natural tree outta the ground, roots 'n' all. He whipped 'round and stood there all spraddle legged and his neck lowered, lookin' at me like he was the bull of the brakes. I done reached down 'n' picked a clod and throwed it at him, 'n' he never twitched. I done reached down 'n' picked up 'nother clod and throwed it at him, and hollered, "Go on," 'n' he took off runnin' down the side of thet corral like winter wind, 'n' he hit the end of thet rope agin, 'n' there we was agin starin' at each other like kids on a playground.

I half-hitched thet rope 'n' strolled real nice kinda close to him, 'n' said, "So how'd ya like thet rope?"

He didn't say nuthin'. He jist took off agin, 'n' this time when he hit the end of thet rope he jist stood there with his hind end to me. So I reached down 'n' picked up 'nother clod and throwed it at him, 'n' said, "Git your hind end outta my face."

He didn't do nuthin'. His disposition has all the flexibility of a iron skillet.

How borin' kin it git? Well, I was glad to see William Hopkins come ridin' up to the corral; I kin tell ya thet, 'cause I'd had 'nough of thet two-year-old fer one day, even if sometimes William Hopkins carries a right fine arrogance around with him. William was ridin' thet sorrel geldin' of his, the one with the white blaze face 'n' white stockings all 'round thet he's so proud of. Thet sorrel was sweatin' pretty fair, and William looked like he had seen sumpthin up a skirt thet surprised him somewhat, his eyes all agate white, and his voice like a nail drawn across slate. "Ray," he hollered, even though I was standin' right there in front of him, "Injuns broke off the rez. There's goin' to be a fight. Let's go."

Well, thet set me back somewhat, but like an idiot, like Uncle Arnie said I was, I said, "Really?" I guess if I was any more gullible, I'd run like sugar.

'N' by thet time Uncle Arnie was standin' there, too, lookin' fer all the world like he'd been fresh dipped in vinegar.

William said, "Shore as hell. Harry Carter, Benjy Jefferson, me 'n' Bob Shafter are goin' to cut 'em off. We figur'd you'd come 'long, too."

Now, there was a thing a man oughta do. Why, there hadn't been no injun fight in least twenty years, thet I knew of, 'n' a man oughta be in one, 'n' I was tired of breakin' thet sorry two-year-old, 'n' like an idiot, I was ready right then. Thet's when Uncle Arnie jist sniffed his nose, 'n' said, "Silliest thing I ever heard. Jist some huntin' party out butcherin' a few antelope, like as not."

"There's a lot of 'em. Headin' this here way, Arnie," William said. He sounded like an old woman havin' a hard time herdin' her chickens.

"Silliest thing I ever heard," Uncle Arnie said.

"They're acallin' the army out. I heard thet," William said.

"They're always sayin' sumpthin', ain't they," Uncle Arnie said, his iris eyes tiny as buttons, and he sniffed his nose agin, 'n' jist walked away, his hands near to touchin' his knees, his legs bowed 'nough to set a banjo 'tween. I heard him say, "Idiots."

"Well, Ray?" William said.

A lotta men made a name fer themselves fightin' injuns, and a man oughta be somebody, so I said, "Lemme git rid of this here two-year-old, 'n' we're on our way."

Well, me 'n' William rode out the next mornin'—I was ridin' thet bay mare, Matilda, 'n' I'll tell ya, she's a lot better to git 'long with then thet kid a hers; she has thet easy walk and trot thet makes ya sleepy jist thinkin' 'bout it, 'n' I don't care what William thinks, I bet Matilda kin outrun thet sorrel a his, 'n' leadin' ol' Jack with thet big canvas tent on him, 'n' 'nough pots and pans fer a whole regiment—toward Three Cripples, and shore 'nough, there was Benjy 'n' Harry 'n' Bob awaitin' fer us, 'n' so we rode on together.

We was headin' fer the ol' Missoury crossin' on the Platte 'bove Delbert Cox's place. That's the crossin' them boys used haulin' supplies to Fort Fetterman from Fort Collins back in the old days, and the reason they call it the Missoury Crossin' is 'cause all them bull whackers was Missouryans, long-haired 'uns, so I ever heard. We went right near where there was a fight in them days, but there wasn't nuthin' these days to see, even though I heard thet back a time there was pieces of burnt wood off'n the wagons and some rusty wheel irons scattered 'bout, but thet was a long time back 'fore my time. It was jist a windy, rocky knoll like any other I ever seed, but we set there fer a full minute, all of us not doin' any talkin' but jist lookin' 'n' thinkin' thet pretty soon we was goin' to be jist as famous as them boys was. Were we ever a bunch of idiots.

William, he done said, "We'll make it good for these here boys," his voice jist like a breeze movin' grass, 'n' we done rode on, all of us silent, thinkin' 'bout them Missouryans baried somewheres back there, 'n' how we was goin' to make things jist dandy fer 'em, like we was some kind of avengers out to make right some incredible mistake that had happened a long time ago.

Finally, come late afternoon, we come to the scarp above the Platte valley. Right here, the Platte's about a foot deep 'n' a hunnert yards wide 'n' there's full breasted cottonwoods thet had their shadders gathered under 'em, 'n' willers along the banks thet seemed to flow with a sound like the scent of honey. Right here, the south side of the river is the gray scarp 'n' the other side is a long, turquoise sagebrush ridge thet comes right down to the water thet was as purple as lupine thet evenin'. It's a raggedy country.

There ain't no crossin' anymore though you kin still see the faint wagon trail, dim like a page in an old and yellowed book. You try to go 'crost here, now, 'n' you'll sink in sand nobody knows how deep, but we figured them injuns wasn't smart 'nough to know 'bout thet, anymore. Least any injun I ever seed. 'Course, I ain't never seed too many. Jist at fair time, 'n' then they're always drunk. I guess there ain't no sich thing as a sober or smart injun.

Well, it was real sharp. We done hobbled our horses 'n' un-packed the two packhorses and stowed the gear 'n' set up thet big white canvas tent of Uncle Arnie's—yep, he done lent it to us, and called us a bunch of idiots, agin—'n' gathered up a lot of firewood and built us a big pit with rocks 'round it fer a fire. Then we done rolled out our bedrolls 'n' put our Winchesters next to us 'n' laid back, 'n' rolled a cigarette.

Yep, it was real sharp, 'bout as good as anythin' kin git, 'specially when I ain't got thet sorry two-year-old on the other end of a rope.

"How many, ya figger?" Benjy asked in thet voice a his'n that sounds like old plank strained. Benjy always looks like he'd been purified in a church with them eyes the color of Blue Bells, innocent like a little girl's.

"How many what?" William asked, his voice slow like it had worn out, but still swollen with his stubborn intolerance.

"Injuns," Benjy said.

"Hunnert," William said.

Well, thet set me back somewhat. A hunnert injuns is a lot, even if they wasn't nuthin' but a bunch of drunks. I mean if a hunnert drunks takes aim and fires, somebody could git hit by accident, even by drunk injuns.

"They ain't no hunnert," Harry said.

"How do you know?" William asked.

"Ain't a hunnert of 'em left," Harry said with a pure assurance.

"Ya didn't answer 'im, Harry," Bob said. Bob sat limply like a used rope against his sand stranded saddle, his gaze hovering some-where near the ends of his booted toes.

"Old Reston said so. He fought 'em," Harry said with a safe

arrogance, jist 'bout like the way thet two-year-old I was breakin' would if he could talk.

Well, thet made me look up somewhat, and William said, "Don't make no difference. We could hold this here crossin' fer a month if we had to. Ain't no injuns comin' cross here, now er any other time, by God."

"I guess yer right 'bout thet," Benjy said, his voice suddenly taking on a reckless noise like a rolling bucket.

"We could whip seven hunnert drunk Sioux," William said.

We was havin' a right sharp time whippin' all them Sioux thet was goin' to show up in a few minutes. Then Benjy asked, "Who's cookie?"

"Good idea, Benjy," I said.

"We been meanin' to talk to ya 'bout thet, Ray," William said, 'n' I got the idea real quick. Well, thet was Jake with me, 'cause Uncle Arnie made me learn to cook when I was jist a kid so I could take care of myself if need be, and I don't mind sayin' I ain't a bad hand at the cook fire.

Hey, we had a feast thet evenin'; Bob done brought some deer thet his mom had canned the last fall, 'n' I had thought to bring a couple cans of store-bought peaches stuffed into my saddlebags, 'n' so we set out there 'n' et thet deer and them peaches and smoked a cigarette.

Jist like sojers, then, we tallied up and split the guard fer the night with William takin' the first watch up to midnight and then me spellin' him 'til daylight, 'n' the others rotatin' the next nights 'til we done had to start all over agin. Thet was William's idea; he somehow kinda 'lected hisself the ramrod, I guess. I don't care; it don't make no nevermind. If'n William wants to do the honors, I say let him, even if it was Harry who talked to ol' Reston 'n' got the deal straight.

So I set out there in the night from midnight to dawn watchin' thet ford as best I could, the river lookin' endless in the moonlight 'n' the trees slidin' their shadders quietly over the ground makin' the night all pintoed. Them's the kinda nights a feller oughta spend. Wasn't no two-year-old hammerhead tryin' to gut me with his hoofs; wasn't no William Hopkins tryin' to run the outfit with his insinuatin' ways. William shook me 'wake come daylight, 'n' said, "Damn good thing they didn't come last night."

"What the hell does that mean?" I asked.

"How long you been asleep?" he asked.

"You see any injuns?" I asked.

"Damn lucky, no," he said.

"I don't neither," I said, and I went back to camp. I don't have to put up with thet kinda sass from any William Hopkins, now ner anyother time.

We all done waited thet mornin'. We spread out through them willers at the edge of the river, but the only thing we had done fought with thet mornin' was them damn deerflies and skeeters, but thet was pretty hot work, what with nary a breeze, 'n' only 'bout middle of the day did some clouds come along to give a shadder or two, clouds like someone had been spinnin' cotton and lost some. The bank of the river looked and felt like there was fever in it.

I couldn't believe it when I heard thet Model T. Kin you imagine how much sense someone has to have to drive a carload of females to a battleground to watch the fireworks? We all done stood up like somehow time had done caught us and wouldn't let go. Thet Model T crawled to the edge of the scarp and set there like some kind of black beetle drying out in the sun. Then, thet fool Billy Milner stood up and waved down to us. Then, all them girls stood up and waved down to us.

Except Laurel Belt. She jist stood there in thet Model T lookin' straight at me, stood there with her hands on her hips, lookin' like she was a real delicate urn, lookin' straight down at me, 'n' I couldn't help but look over to William, 'n' he smiled back at me like he jist sucked a sugar tit, but 'fore he could say somethin', I headed fer camp with everbody else a follerin' me, like I was some kind of a magnet. They hopped outta thet Model T, 'n' come down the scarp, Nellie Milner, Billy's sister, 'n' Lucy Jefferson, Benjy's sister, 'n' Karen Fife from over Wagonhound way, carryin' baskets. Laurel, she wasn't carrin' nothin' but her skinny self, lookin' fer all the world like a thin and tender blade of grass noddin' in a breeze, the way she moved her hips.

I couldn't believe it. They had done come fer a picnic right in the middle of a injun fight.

Laurel has a kinda frail grace 'bout her like a pasque flower, 'n' her skin's the color of ripe meadow. She has fiercely opal eyes, 'n' a smile like a sickle of moon. When she talks her mouth opens like she was suddenly surprized. She's jist like a honey tree 'n' warm as summer. When Laurel come down there, she jist took me by a hand 'n' led me back toward the river, 'n' I knew I wasn't like myself atall, really, anymore, like I was changin', like my feet and my arms really weren't me anymore, and that my whole body was changin', too. I could feel ever' cell in my body changin', 'n' I felt hot like a winter, whiskey toddy that was seethin' up through my chest 'n' through my neck 'n' into my head, and wherever it went I couldn't see or hear anymore, like I was drownin' in hot molasses, 'n' then I didn't know how to breathe anymore. It was like I was blind 'n' deef, 'n' I had changed so much I wasn't really me atall anymore, so I couldn't do anythin' but let whoever I had become do whatever he was agonna do. I knew ever'body could feel me beatin' like I was a huge, exposed heart. William knew it, too, and I think Bob done knowed it, too, but I don't think anyone else did.

She never said nothin' till we was almost there, 'n' then she turned 'n' looked up at me with them speckled eyes 'n' said, "Too bad we cain't do nothin', ain't it?" Her voice is kinda like two pieces of new, unoiled leather bein' rubbed 'gether, but when she don't talk she's pretty nice.

When she starts on to you, she starts with a determination thet don't leave no doubt of her purpose.

"We kin go down river a spell." I knew I sounded like I had jist run a race.

"No, we cain't, Ray, sugar. I ain't gonna give it to ya right here in front of ever'body. Jesus, Lucy 'n' Benjy is sich prudes, they'd tell ever'body we was doin' it."

"We kin go further."

"They's gonna be a dance in Esterbrook in jist two weeks, 'n' we kin meet there like we did the last time," she purred lazily 'n' pitifully like she was mournin' fer a child or somethin'.

"I'll shore be there, Laurel," I said. I felt like I was standin' in honey.

"Drive thet Model T a your'n, sugar."

"I shore will, Laurel."

When we was havin' thet there picnic, William he done come over to Laurel and tried to make up to her. I jist took Laurel by her hand 'n' took her up to the Model T, 'n' we stood there 'til ever'body come up. Later, William he done said, "Damn, yer touchy 'bout her." He looked fer all the world like a feller who jist been bit by his dog 'n' didn't quite understand jist why.

"She's givin' free milk, 'n' I ain't loanin' her," I told him, 'n' thet's all there was to thet.

Thet night it rained. Thet was when we figured out why Uncle Arnie hadn't been so particular 'bout loanin' us his tent. Wasn't long 'fore some drops of water was keepin' time to the thunder. We done set out a couple of tin cups, but they filled up pretty quick, 'n' then I lit a lamp, 'n' we counted fourteen leaks and five tin cups, two pots, 'n' a fryin' pan, which left us on the uphill side of the climb. The wind jist kinda caressed thet old tent but ever' once in a while it gave her a real squeeze, 'n' then I'll be damned but she didn't come unhitched on the wind side.

Thet ol' tent lifted her skirt with a sound like the insides of a hardware store was sick, and then suddenly it was like the bottom of a lake done give out right above us. There I was tryin' to hold on to my blanket with one hand while the wind was tryin' to snap it like we was runnin' wild horses and hoppin' 'round on one foot tryin' to git my boot on with the other hand before it filled up and pulled me under and right then the wind blowed me right over on top of William, and I lost the damn blanket, and if thet weren't enough, I had to put up with William cussin' me and sayin', "Dammnit, Ray, git off me; ya got yer elbow right in my belly and yer breath is terrible," 'n' thet was when the whole dang thing went off down river in the night 'n' rain, long with most everthin' else we had with us.

Benjy he kept hollerin', "Ketch thet tent! Ketch thet tent!" Hell, ya couldn't a caught thet tent to save yer soul from Hell, 'n' fer all we knowed right then it coulda been up a cottonwood or down in the bottom of the river or halfway to Glendo. Harry he kept hollerin' fer us to run fer it. By God, I weren't goin' nowhere till I got my boot on. I got better sense than to be runnin' bare-footed all over hell in the middle of the night in thet country. Why there's rattlesnakes all over thet place, and thet's all we needed right then was for some damn fool to git snake bit by some waterlogged rattlesnake thet had been driv outta his hole was unhappy about it, 'n', anyway, I don't know where we was goin' to run to, 'cause any place you sloshed there was jist water.

The only thing we was missin' right then was a smelly damn dog to beat us with his damn wet tail. I don't how we coulda' missed not havin' one with us, but somehow we did.

Come mornin' I guess we probably looked so dilapidated we woulda' been depressin' fer mules to look at.

Next mornin' ever'thin' was wet. All our beddin' 'n' clothes, and one of them hunnert year drizzles set in on us. Wasn't a stick of dry firewood anywhere near where we was, 'n' all we done was stand in a huddle with our ponchos over us 'n' shiver, 'n' figure no injun in his right mind, no matter how damn dumb or drunk he was, was gonna go out in this stuff. Thet night we didn't even bother to put out any guards. We jist stood 'n' got waterlogged 'nough so water wouldn't stay on us, but jist runoff. Nobody much cared whether we was attacked or not.

Well, ever'thin' was goin' to hell in a basket, 'n' ever'one of us knowed it, too. We had been overcome with an infectious gloom. "Let's go," said Benjy. Say what you want 'bout Benjy, he was the bravest of us, no doubt.

"We ain't been relieved," William said.

"'N' this here ain't no relief," I said.

"Let's go," Benjy said, agin.

"We oughta vote," William said. (Vote, hell. All he was tryin' to do was git his smart ass outta a mess.)

"Ever'one wants to go, say so," I said.

Ever'one said so, so we went. 'Fore we got back to Three Cripple crossin', we done rode on to Dutch Holliman, who was ridin' thet little dun mare of his. He done looked at us like he was waitin' fer 'nother half of a letter to be read to him so he'd understand what it was he was supposed to know. "You fellers been fishin'?" he finally asked.

"We was at Missoury Crossin' waitin' to cut them injuns off," William said with thet seemingly spontaneous impudence that he carries with him.

Dutch he looked up at thet forlorn sky, 'n' then looked back at us, 'n' he said, "Ya'll mean them up toward Hawk Sprangs?"

"I reckon," I said.

"Them?" Dutch done said.

"Thet warparty," William done said.

"Warparty?" Dutch done said.

"They was a hunnert of 'em," William said.

"They was two old men, one young buck, three kids and two women ridin' a wagon hitched to two old horses, 'n' they whipped all hell outta Mike Cardigan, who elected hisself some kinda injun hunter fer some silly reason, 'n' ten of his men, 'n' thet was a week ago."

Now you see why I cain't go? I cain't never go to a dance agin or out anywhere's in front of people. Why, they'd laugh themselves to death at me if I did thet, 'n' I cain't be responsible fer so many deaths due to laughin'. Anyways, Uncle Arnie he done told me he'd show me how to braid horsehair into ropes and bridles 'n' sich. Now that's somethin' a man can do to make a name fer hisself, 'n' it shore as hell beats breakin' thet sorry, Goddamn, two-year-old hammerhead, too, by God.

Bootleggers

One

The adventure began so ordinarily we had no warning of what was happening.

Of course, we were incautious then, too. And terrible things happened.

Anyway, my cousin Jeremy—his grandson is your cousin Jerry— and I crouched against the corner of the log bunkhouse. Suddenly, Tom Wathford, the foreman, bolted through the open doorway dragging Lefty by his hair after him. Lefty was reeling after Tom, and Tom was yelling, "Goddamn ya, Lefty, ya drunked-upped son- of-a-bitch," over and over, as though he had misplaced any other words, and Lefty was weakly moaning all the time, "Goddamn, Tom, stop it. Goddamn that hurts." Tom dragged Lefty all the way to the water trough and shoved his head down in the water, and Lefty's arms were waving like he might be trying to fly and he kept stamping his bare feet up and down in the dirt. Tom just kept holding his head under the water.

I looked at Jeremy and he looked at me, and he said, "He's goin' ta drown 'im."

"Maybe so," I answered.

Finally, Tom jerked Lefty up, shoved him away, and said, "Now, Goddamnit! Git dressed and git ta work." He stomped away toward the house and Lefty just stood there limp as grass and staring after him, speechless and bedraggled as a tuckered-out dog.

It was as though all this were an instinctual action, something that could not have been altered by any thought by either man, as strong as any mating sacrament.

That it happened with annual punctuality had no bearing on any one time that it happened, each time being treated with singular gravity, individually and intensely. It precisely punctuated the season, and for either man to ignore the event would have been a breach of honor beyond the comprehension of the other, so habitual had both it and they become. Uncle Pate would wait with a patience that only could have been understood by a deity for the event, now certainly a social one, to manifest itself.

The house then had just been framed. The great logs had been dragged by horse, carried by wagon and squared by man and then set one upon another. Now, they were covered with thin, white boards at the urging of your great grandmother, Winibeth, who after a wifehood of childbearing and improbable and unreasonable acquiescence, finally, suddenly like a late winter storm, had demanded of Uncle Pate a home rather than a fortress. Consequently, the huge, log blockhouse had been remolded into a great, white cake with frosted towers that watched reprovingly with its several tinted eyes those rhapsodic days. Aunt Winibeth even had forced Uncle Pate to cover the logs and chinking with plaster and paper, which gave the rooms a fairytale quality, luminescent and delicate.

All this, of course, with the exception of Uncle Pate's office, which, with a stubbornness as willful as any Aunt Winibeth claimed, he maintained if not in egotistical martial splendor then at least in memory of his personal sacrifice to his wife for the remainder of his home. He would sit, surrounded by the great deer and elk antlers he had proudly mounted about himself, at his desk in the large room off the parlor. The room still held the exuberant smell of pine, which was mingled with the autumn smell of cigar smoke, and, for that matter, appeared as through some undefinable haze through which the sunlight from the single window drifted to the cherrywood floor. He sat in his straight-backed carved oak chair at his heavy oak desk that looked like a large, sepia beast that finally had died there in the middle of the room. Upon it he carelessly had thrown papers and ashtrays and other odds and ends, including matches and pencils and the remains of tiny dead flowers that once had been inspirations but always became only forgotten dust, as though he had no respect at all for the poor animal. Obviously, he had even decided not to allow its burial but only its petrification under an accumulation of corral dust.

Tom Wathford, who always brought with him into the house and to the office not only the clean and metallic tannic odors of horses and cattle but also the aura of senescent parchment, was reserved the right to inform Uncle Pate that the annual and waited-for moment finally had arrived. Tom always stood like an aspen dressed for winter in front of Uncle Pate, and there he would wait, his hands folded one over the other, with a braided, leather quirt, as shiny as a floor worn from use, hanging from his right wrist, until Uncle Pate would look up with an expression of mild surprise as though the apparition of a nearly forgotten acquaintance had just appeared. Then, looking down at his desk, or at least at something near his desk, and smoothing his elegant and lustrous black hair with a small and compact fist, he would point to the aromatic cedar cigar box as if brushing a bothersome fly away. Tom would open the box on cue as though he had practiced the motion beforehand—which he certainly had with a yearly punctuality that could have appeased a teacher—and take a cigar and put it in his vest pocket.

"What is it now?" Uncle Pate would ask, knowing the answer as

well as he knew each old log or rack of antlers or rifle or pistol seques-
tered in the high, glass-fronted case he kept locked in his office, but
this also was a scene in the drama to be played without divergence
from a script written—no, not written, but memorized to become
a folktale.

"Two riders came in drunk last night, Pate," Tom said, his voice
sounding like a wagon wheel moving through grass, the feigned dis-
interest only another element of the play now unfolding like a dawn
before a watching plain.

"Who were they?" Uncle Pate looked up now, officiously with
great presumption, while Tom said brazenly, "Won't tell ya, Pate.
Won't have ya firin' good men out from under me."

"By God, I own this ranch, Tom."

"You own it, Pate, but, by God, I have ta ramrod it."

Uncle Pate would hesitate, then, until it seemed that the silence
could wait no longer to be filled before something probably profane
would happen, and then he would say as he said every year, "Have it
your way, then. You'll have trouble over it. How the hell did they get
the stuff?"

"Well, Pate, they didn't say, rightly, buy I s'pose ya know the
answer well as I do," Tom would say, still standing, a tacit equality
in his every slight movement or nod of his head, that quality of famil-
iarity between the two men, the one knowing he needed to have that
or, at least, wanted to have that, and other conceding, not reluctantly
or even grudgingly, but consenting as one might to a conspiratorial
sin of pleasure.

"I s'pose I do. God knows I've tried to be lenient with him all
these years."

"All of us know that, Pate."

"Let him sit out there on my land."

"A long time, Pate."

"Let him do business without interference."

"You always been a man of goodness, Pate."

"And this is what he does to me."

"Ever'one knows it's a crime."

"Well, then, I guess we know what to do."

"S'pose we do, Pate."

"We'll leave at daybreak."

"I'll have the horses waitin'."

It was not necessary to ride horses. We much easier could have taken the truck, but that would have been a preemptive abrogation not agreed upon by either man in the drama, the two principal actors, Uncle Pate and Old Man Boudreaux. And, if we had taken the truck, we would have had to walk the final two miles up the wagon road, because several years before Old Man Boudreaux had spirited away from Roaring Fork Creek two adult beaver and put them among the delicious willows of what today is called Boudreaux's Draw to build dams to block the road to vehicles that unimaginative revenue agents habitually used to track down bootleggers who they must have considered to be nothing other than dolts, and neither Uncle Pate nor Tom—I knew, and know now even better than I did then, at least I understand better today—would have walked anywhere if they could have ridden a horse, since anything, as far as they were concerned, that could not be done from a horse's back probably wasn't worth doing, anyway. For us to have driven the truck was not even considered.

We left the ranch buildings when they still were dark shadows like the silhouettes of ships on a black sea, the four of us, Uncle Pate, Tom, my cousin, Jeremy, and myself, Jeremy and I making our first trip onto the stage simply because Uncle Pate had decided that it was time to introduce new blood, his blood, or, at least, family blood, to the yearly rite, for us to begin to memorize our lines, like neophytes, children sitting and listening to a shaman or medicine man instruct us. Jeremy and I had been given no instructions at all much less a script, but were expected to somehow naturally assume our roles with the instincts we had inherited, riding through a sapphire twilight, only the ring of spur rowels like a Christmas carol heard from a great distance and the sound of the horses' hooves on the hard and dusty ground like distant axe strokes for an accompaniment.

Old Man Boudreaux's face had an expression of a person upon whom some replete and ultimate terror had just descended. He gestured like a fish just thrown on a deck, while your great grandfather's immobility appeared to be an unalterable and eternal and undeniable property that always had been, was now, and always would be suffered. When Old Man Boudreaux finally did speak, his voice groaned and creaked like an old floor.

"By Goddamn, Pate, I'll be damned ta hell ya will."

"By God, I'll be damned if I don't," your great grandfather, my uncle, Pate answered, as if he were delivering a theological tenet rather than what it actually was, a courtly gesture, a learned line politely returned on its cue, one that had been delivered more times than probably either man could instantly have remembered. Nonetheless, it was a reply that had to be given or neither man would have remembered which line came next in this melodramatic sequence that by this time had become an historical monument to meaningless repetition, like a religious festival, a rite or ceremony of which the beginning, middle, and present had no meaning at all to anyone anymore, but still was something that had to be practiced and recited for its own sake.

It was then that we all heard Calvin and saw him, glimpsed him. He looked like a bare tree suddenly and magically given the jubilant quality of movement. We watched him flapping awkwardly over the ground, not touching it, really, but skimming it like a rock thrown to skip on still water, running down the draw. Then we heard him again uttering a sound like a gurgle. We all were mesmerized by Calvin, not understanding why he didn't fall, watching him as though he were part of some miracle happening before us, as though we were anticipating his fall that would have allowed us to come to our senses, and that until his fall, we were not allowed to either think or move. Finally, Old Man Boudreaux said, "Oh, shit," very quietly, as if he had been given a divine insight to the future, and then, this time loudly, "Oh, shit," when the realization of the situation became evident to all us at the same time.

"Well, hell," Uncle Pate said, as though he had just discovered a broken fence wire that would have to be mended from the ground.

"The horses," Tom said. He did not have to speak to either Jeremy or me; we understood the instruction instantly, and we turned and ran up the few yards to the top of the ridge, and saw instantly that we had been too late, so we stopped and turned and watched as Calvin kept somehow above the rocks and fallen timber as though he were suspended by invisible strings and moved like a puppet over the ground, the sow, like a landslide, coming after him, stumbling over the rocks and fallen pines that lay like the kind of sticks children play with, scattered across the draw as though thrown there by an angry god, and the two cubs, one black like onyx, the other brown as new mud, following her, looking like two acrobats at play, spilling and tumbling over and through the obstacles on their own haphazard paths. Old Man Boudreaux wonderously found the suppressed motion available to him, and he was running toward the cabin, yelling at Calvin, "Don't run here, Goddamnit! Run that way!" throwing an arm in an unintelligible direction away from him. Both Uncle Pate and Tom were still standing where we had left them, watching, too, but like disinterested parties to a calamity that was taking place before them, as though both were merely examining a new phenomena that wouldn't have any effect on either of them.

Old Man Boudreaux disappeared into the log cabin and Calvin, who had not bothered to even attempt to follow Old Man Boudreaux's inarticulate directions, followed him into the cabin. We heard Old Man Boudreaux yell at Calvin, "Goddamnit, I told you not to follow me!" and then we saw Old Man Boudreaux come away from the cabin with his rifle in his hand with Calvin sprinting and flapping past him up the hill like a goose herding goslings.

The sow was in the cabin and we could hear her groaning as if she had been put under an unbearable weight, and then we heard Tom yell, "Go on, damnit, get the hell away!" and we saw him kick the black cub and send it rolling over and over down the draw, the brown cub following the black one, both of them squealing. The sow rushed out of the front door of the cabin, stumbled, and sprawled in the dirt in front of the cabin, staggered to her feet and, still groaning like a dental patient, charged after her cubs, the three of them making a noise like an untuned band.

Old Man Boudreaux ran from behind the cabin and raised his rifle and fired, the sound from the old Winchester like a large dry board suddenly split, and him yelling, "Get the hell outta here, Goddamnit!"

Calvin retrieved his courage and came and stood next to Old Man Boudreaux, looking over him at the sow and her cubs as they smashed into a wall of willows, amazingly not even bending a branch in the process. "Hell, I could uh got her," he said.

Old Man Boudreaux looked up at Calvin and said, "You couldn't uh got her if she 'uz in a box."

"You shoulda got her for what she done ta the still," Calvin offered as a possible inducement to Old Man Boudreaux to try again.

"What the hell does that mean?"

"When I got there she and them cubs had et all the mash and broke everthin'. They uz drunkern hell."

"Jesus, Goddamnit to Christ!" Old Man Boudreaux yelled, and he threw his rifle down in the dust. He looked over at Uncle Pate, who had not bothered to even shift his feet during the episode but who had according to his expression remained only a member of an audience listening to a boring recital. "Well, Goddamnit, Pate, ya cain't hurt my still now, by God, ya cain't."

Uncle Pate didn't even bother to answer him. He finally moved just enough to look back up the hill at Jeremy and me still standing like dumb statues, and said, "Bring the horses."

"We cain't," Jeremy answered.

Both Uncle Pate and Tom stared at us for quite some time before Uncle Pate said, "Damnit." It was all he said, and he said it the way a preacher might say "Amen" at the end of an appropriate sermon. He just started walking back to the ranch with Tom following him. Behind us we could hear for some time Old Man Boudreaux laughing as though he just had discovered how to do it and was making up for most of a deprived lifetime of not knowing how to laugh.

During haying season Jeremy and I already had been told before the fact that we were going to go with Uncle Pate and Tom and Lefty to Casper to pick up the new bull. The new Hereford bull had been purchased a year before at Goodland. Uncle Pate and Tom had driven to Wheatland to inspect the yearling bulls at a ranch near there, and Uncle Pate had bought the yearling bull then, but he also had purchased another year for the bull, so the owners kept it until this summer, and then they shipped it by rail to Casper for Uncle Pate. I suppose that Uncle Pate's taking us to Casper with him to pick up the new bull was similar to his taking us with him to Old Man Boudreaux's, although Uncle Pate did not tell us, or anyone else of whom I know, that he had any reason for doing this. We certainly did not think of a reason for going to Casper with Uncle Pate. The process involved in such a concept was beyond our recognition. The immediacy of the event itself was as much as we could possibly understand.

We both had been to Casper before, and we each easily envisioned that which we knew of the town, its bustling downtown and its tree-lined streets and large homes, some of them just as sumptuous as Uncle Pate and Aunt Winibeth's white, crenellated ranch house, but without the walls thick with huge, plaster-covered ponderosa logs, which made us think of the town houses as nothing more than fancy frostings covering hollow cakes. There were large brick homes there that did make us pause or turn to look, though. If that would have been all of which we thought of Casper, we would not have been quite so eager to go pick up a new bull, for there was really nothing in the cars and trucks or houses that could interest us, since we already had seen those before and more than once.

It was the conjured visions of the delectable untouchables that excited our imaginations. The things of which we only had heard about from other boys and from the other cowboys were barrooms, gambling dens, and whorehouses along Casper's vaunted Sandbar. We wished to glimpse these things as others had done before us.

An idea is only as good as the person who nurtures it. It is only as good as the person is at sorting out its intricacies. How an idea can affect oneself is important, but how an idea might affect others is even more important; that is called ethical behavior; it is the essence of morality. Unfortunately, reason is most often the servant of some desire, as it is the handmaiden of one's will to do something. Only a person who is good at freeing reason from some constricting selfishness can call an idea good, and the more one is pressed by an economic necessity, the less time one has for reason. But it is necessary for one to look inside himself, to reflect upon his nature, to consult his obvious interests, and, then, most importantly, to consider the object of people. Then one can understand the difference between a good idea and bad idea.

Unfortunately, reasoning is an intoxication, and imbibing too deeply of the brew without a certain capacity for such a draft usually leaves one with only its sour dregs.

I know how the idea was born within us. Lefty rode beside us while we were mending the south fence. He sat on his horse with an impudent indifference, wearing lassitude as though it were a robe. With a preciseness marked by its particular carelessness, he looped his reins around his saddle horn, swung his left leg over his horse's neck, pulled out a sack of tobacco and a thin slip of paper, and made himself a mathematically rolled cigarette. He did all that before he even looked down at us.

We had not bothered to look up at him, either, since it was accepted by the three of us that we, Jeremy and I, were the common laborers and hardly worth his even starting a conversation with since we were on the ground, and he was not, which as good as made him genetically superior to us, and all of us knew that no matter how long Lefty sat there watching us, he was not going to dismount. To have stepped down from his horse would have been both indecorous for him and condescending and embarrassing to us.

It would have been an intrinsically impossible gesture for him to make.

He sat there in his temporary repose looking permanently elastic and as though some discouragement had marred him for the remainder of his life, and we had no reason to doubt at all that he was not ever going to change, because as far as we were concerned nothing had ever happened to Lefty that was not at least depressing. It seemed as though he carried in his saddlebags a set of steps that he could limber at any time and over which he could stumble. Lefty was disheveled both mentally and morally.

"Fixin' fence," he finally said, his voice purring with an indolent presumptuousness. His words seemed to pass through Texas honey before being heard.

"What does it look like, Lefty?" Jeremy said, as though he were making an acute and daring accusation, his voice like two pieces of rusted iron rubbing.

"No need to git scratchy, Jere. I ain't no tick, even if you ain't but a pup."

"I ain't the pup you think I am, Lefty," Jeremy said, his voice still holding that irritating rasping sound that made one's skin cringe.

"Shore you ain't, Jere." Lefty had a smile like a fingernail.

"What does that mean, Lefty?" Jeremy said, and both Lefty and I knew that Jeremy was not going to back down or away, now that he had convinced himself that Lefty had actually voiced the insult—the difference between he and Lefty or any fence mender and any cowboy—so that it now trembled between them like aspen leaves caught in a river of wind, so that the difference between them no longer was only an implied principle but now was an actual menace.

"Nuthin', I reckon, Jere," he finally said, but Jeremy even then wouldn't let go of it, not now, not once Lefty had thrown the accusation of his disregard at him, and Jeremy said, "Then lay off me, you son-of-a-bitch."

I know that neither Jeremy nor I moved during the moment in which Lefty disappeared from his saddle and hit Jeremy. Neither Jeremy nor I had ever been witnesses to such movement and the very velocity of his execution captivated both of us better than any circus act. We had watched from the edge of a plain as if we were anticipating a vision to form before us. Then I could not nor now can I see any specific action, any defining second that sets itself apart from the whole. Lefty was as fluid as a stream. "Now, goddamn you, Pup, by God, you be damn careful how you talk to a man," Lefty said, his voice taking on a new aspect, one of demand.

Jeremy lay there, a red welt spreading like dawn across one side of his face, his legs and arms still stretched and straight just the way they had been when Lefty had suddenly hit him. His eyes were blinking like evening stars, and, with a whine like a broken axle, he said, "You hit me."

Lefty knelt down next to him and said, "Well, you figured that out, so you cain't be too bad hurt. Gimme yer hand."

Lefty pulled Jeremy to his feet and Jeremy shook his head and put his hand to where the red welt had grown to cover the side of his face, making him look as though he suddenly were blushing, as though he had been discovered practicing the proposal of a marriage.

"You'll be all right, I reckon," Lefty said, and he walked back to his horse and mounted. "Why don't you boys come on along. I got some business to settle up over the ridge."

"We got to fix this fence," I said.

"I reckon it'll wait," Lefty said.

"Uncle Pate'll raise Cain if we don't," Jeremy said.

"He won't know it if ya don't tell him," Lefty said. "Let's go."

"You ain't the one who'll catch it," Jeremy said.

"No, I ain't, and neither will you if ya keep yer mouth shut. This old fence can wait," his voice again lapping lazily on a beach. His hands, as big as pitchforks, I noticed for the first time, were holding his saddle horn, his head bowed as though he were deep in a meditation that had nothing to do with us or what was around us.

"Let us just finish this splice," Jeremy said. He had to say at least that; he had to gather some self-respect back around himself, make some kind of effort to show both of us that he was able to make a decision by himself, but he already had surrendered to the older man; no, not given up, but acquiesced, accepted the agreement without saying, "Yes, we'll go."

"I can set here," Lefty said.

You see how easily a conspiracy happens? Of course, both Jeremy and I were susceptible. We were young, and certainly younger than Lefty, with all that being young implies, imbued with an amazing naivety bolstered with a self indulgence that verged on insanity with a complete disdain of either implications or retributions, other than the possible but unlikely uncovering of the fact that we had not completed what we had been sent to do. We easily rationalized that we would fulfill our obligation to Uncle Pate, only at a later time, but nonetheless finish what we had started to do, thereby correcting our miniscule, as we then saw it, indiscretion. And so we followed along behind Lefty, not being led by Lefty, but agreeing to be a part of whatever business he had to settle, which joined all of us into a secrecy, a bond, unspoken, and if not recognized at least felt like a slight change in a breeze even by Jeremy and I.

It actually was no surprise to us that Lefty rode to Old Man Boudreaux's place. We thought that we also were within the confidence of the terrible and delicious secret—at least, that Lefty visited Old Man Boudreaux occasionally, and that he had been one of the two riders who had precipitated this year's grand play, a fact that was pretended to be concealed from Uncle Pate by Tom, another part of the spectacle, but known by Uncle Pate as surely as he knew the conventionalities of his favorite horse. Even though Uncle Pate knew, and he had, who the two riders were, he could not have fired them because without them there would have been no spring, which meant that he was indebted to them, tacitly, of course, and Tom also knew this, so the entire episode between them, Uncle Pate and Tom, was only another scene memorized and politely played.

Because you are young, you can imagine the very palatable taste of the morsel of unuttered acceptance by others in a hidden fact, its very succulence and lusciousness filling your every pore with a sugary idleness.

Old Man Boudreaux scrutinized the situation with small, black eyes like September chokecherries. His eyes flicked over us in circles like a snake's tongue. He filled the silence in front of his cabin with suspicion until it seemed the air must soon begin to crackle.

"Why?" he asked Lefty, his voice pitched like a saw, unsonorous and irritating, his arms flinging themselves as though he suddenly had been surrounded by gnats.

"'Why,' what?" Lefty asked.

"Why them?"

"They'll be all right, I reckon." Lefty knew we would be. At that moment we could not go tell Uncle Pate that we had visited Old Man Boudreaux anymore than we could have exacted a spirit from a séance.

"This here's a mistake; ya'll see; that damned old man—no offense meant to yer uncle, I forgot yer name, my young friend..."

"Dennis," I said.

"...yes, Dennis, you are a fine boy, as I'm sure yer cousin, Jeree..., what is it? Oh, yes, Jeremy, is, I'm sure, but ya see if that damned old man, 'scuse me again, the old gentleman, finds that ya've been ta see me, he'll destroy me. He'll burn my still; this is the one thing he'll not tolerate. He'll make me move. I've nothing but what ya see, with the exception of the still, of course, but I can't have that here at the cabin, obviously, or the agents would have destroyed me long ago."

"Take it easy, Frenchy," Lefty said. "I said it'd be Jake. The 'Old Gentleman' ain't goin' to know they was here atall."

Old Man Boudreaux made a snort like a bull in rut, and he said, "Yeah, sure, I'll put my life in yer hands. Ya cain't hold a cup of coffee on a Sunday morning."

He looked back at Jeremy and I. "Ya won't tell him, will ya?"

"Nossir," Jeremy said and I shook my head to let him know that I certainly agreed with Jeremy that under no circumstances that I could foresee at the time would I tell Uncle Pate that I had been anywhere near Old Man Boudreaux's place.

"What'd I tell ya?" Lefty said.

"They're children. They'll say anythin' ta let anyone know they've done somethin' they shouldn't," Old Man Boudreaux said.

"Whatever they might be, Frenchy, they ain't liars," Lefty said. "They jist give ya their word on it."

"I'll still worry. I can do that, if I want to."

"I shore wouldn't do nuthin' to try to stop ya if that's what ya wanted to do, Frenchy."

"That, probably, is the only thing I'll have out of this. What do ya want?"

"A bottle for me and my pards," Lefty said.

"Oh, my God," Old Man Boudreaux said. His voice sounded flat as though he were standing behind a door, as though a beloved aunt had just died. "Yer goin' to give 'em whiskey?"

"I reckon I'll take most if it, Frenchy."

Neither Jeremy nor I could offer an opinion. We had been neither left out nor left behind. We had been brought along, involved beyond our experience to extricate ourselves, accepting Lefty as the spokesman for all of us, and even if we had ventured so little as a theory, neither man would have even nodded, so intent on the struggle and its suggestions were they. It would have been a contest of wills had not the outcome have been so obvious. Lefty had won by then. Old Man Boudreaux had to give Lefty a bottle, because if he didn't, his imagination was capable of visualizing the possible damage of the denial, and this thought in Old Man Boudreaux's mind overrode any sensible conclusion on his part, and Lefty knew it, the same way he had known that entering us into the play was the safest thing that he could do for himself.

"I'll sell ya a bottle," Old Man Boudreaux said. He sounded like a bellows released.

"Kind of figured yamight, Frenchy," Lefty said just the way anyone might have said "Good morning" to a stranger.

Old Man Boudreaux came out of his cabin with a glass bottle that would have seemed at a glance to have contained nothing more potent than spring water and nothing more, and Lefty disdained having to lean down from his horse to hand Old Man Boudreaux a silver dollar in exchange for the bottle of moonshine.

"Well, Frenchy, we shore thank ya for passin' the time a day with us, but we gotta git back ta work. These here boys gotta job ta finish up for the 'Old Gentleman.'"

When we left Old Man Boudreaux, he looked like a deflated bellows.

Later that afternoon, when Jeremy and I had finally finished our responsibility to Uncle Pate, Lefty allowed us a sip of Old Man Boudreaux's concoction—another bond between the three of us, one that melded us together in a jovial and stealthy camaraderie of connivance that was both quietly ebullient and mellowly golden—which left in our mouths and tucked up just under our noses a slight exaltation, as though we had somehow been raised to our tiptoes by an unseen string.

"Ya can sell this stuff in Casper fer two bucks a bottle," Lefty said.

Two

Neither Jeremy nor I spoke of the idea in direct terms. There was no reason to because we both had understood from the beginning just what the idea was and vaguely what was necessary in order for the idea to become a reality. However, there was reason not to speak of it in clarified terms, and so we discussed the idea lazily and unassertively but with an exaggerated dedication. If we had dared to speak of the idea aloud we would have been committed to it forever, and that, of course, also would have meant that we would have stepped beyond any threshold we had ever previously imagined. To have verbally in clear words uttered the idea would have boldly signified not just to ourselves but to everyone around us that we had chosen of our own volition to become unfaithful celibates, disregarding our own particular ritual to which we were devoted by all our learning and experience.

There are no degrees of traitors. Either one is or one is not.

And so we would lie awake in the darkness, side by side on the brass-framed feather mattress bed in the turret. At least that is what we called the room because from the outside it looked just like a turret in a picture, shimmering and round and tall and pointed with three small windows that we would open at night so the breeze streams, limpid and silver with stardust, would flow over us. We would tentatively and furtively discuss the idea, latently recognizing it as a variable quandary, because that is just what it was, producing for us not only the question surrounding the tangible idea, but also suggesting the obvious intangible that we were going to set ourselves apart, if we could just determine how to carry out the idea.

"Jeremy?" I asked.

"Yeah, Denny."

"How?"

"I don't know how. I cain't think of how."

"We gotta have money first."

"Well, we ain't got any of that."

"What then?"

"I don't know."

"We cain't steal it."

"Nope. Then we'd really be in for it."

"So, how?"

"Damnit, Denny, I don't know how."

"I don't, neither, Jere."

For us the problem was unsolvable. Whenever we talked about the idea, we were always left feeling as though we had been late for an appointment and had missed whatever it was we were to learn.

We had seduced ourselves through our passionate dalliance with the idea so far that when Lefty said, "We goin' ta take a ride today," we could not abstain, turn away at that moment from the idea, even though both of us knew we should, and that the moment to do so was then. We both knew that when we had accompanied Lefty to Old Man Boudreaux's, we had committed ourselves to Lefty, and in the time between that trip and this day, we had come to understand that we would go the next time, too. Singular commission usually leads to an epidemic.

So, once again we rode quietly to Old Man Boudreaux's, and when we reined up in front of his cabin that was rotting like a brown mushroom in the shadow of the ponderosas, Lefty said, "This'll be the last trip, Frenchy."

"My God, Lefty, ya shouldn't a brought 'em with ya. This was our deal. Now you're goin' ta have everyone know about it. I told ya you were askin' fer trouble when ya brought 'em here the first time, and now ya do it a second time. Ya ain't got good sense, Lefty, and we'll pay like hell, you wait and see."

"You let me worry 'bout that, Frenchy. Bring it out."

"You boys know what will happen, now? Huh? You git caught with this and the Old Gentleman's goin' ta git all of us. He'll put all of us outta business. You wait and see."

"Don't worry, Frenchy. I done thought this out real good fer a long time," Lefty said.

"I don't want ya ta think, damnit, Lefty. That's when things don't go too good."

"I ain't never let ya down, Frenchy."

"You ain't never let me up, neither."

"Bring the stuff," Lefty said, his voice still as smooth as sugar syrup, as though he were offering a condolence to a mourner.

Old Man Boudreaux opened his mouth to speak but he had suddenly forgotten how to form words, and with his arms gesturing with a mysterious urgency, he went into his cabin and came back with a box of twelve bottles of moonshine—all of them just like the bottle that Lefty had bought before—which Lefty divided among us, the three of us, four bottles to each of us, two in each of our saddlebags. Old Man Boudreaux came behind him and stuffed wads of old newspaper in our saddlebags to pad the bottles, the expression on his face that of a man who has seen his fate and has lost all hope of any possible redemption, as if he were always under some form of immutable discouragement, only this time Lefty didn't give Old Man Boudreaux any money.

Jeremy and I accepted the situation. Actually, we had accepted it a long time before, even longed for it, so that now this moment was only what we had been waiting for, yearning for, the past weeks, the improbable fulfillment of our idea, which both of us, though not surprised to realize, were going to share not just with Old Man Boudreaux but also with Lefty, to whom we were now indebted and wedded to as surely as if we had ourselves proposed the union.

When we reached the top of the ridge above the draw where Old Man Boudreaux's cabin squatted, Lefty said, "You pups ain't got nuthin' ta worry 'bout, neither. Ya jist leave everthin' ta me. We're gonna' split it up 'n' have a hell of a toot in Casper."

And there it was. Jeremy and I had everything we needed for the idea to come to such palpitating fruition. We had allowed ourselves to be seduced by our own mistress, we had imagined our necessity, and we had the time to allow the idea to wander and leaven. And we had had assistance, without which we would not have succeeded. Lefty was like a golden leaf, shimmering and effervescent, but like a fall leaf, he, no more than Jeremy and I, was able to see into the future beyond his immediate selfishness and will, as though some part of him somehow had failed to mature or he was unable to achieve enough experience to perceive faint ripplings across a windless pond. And so we—the three of us, insoluable, now—rode ahead in this mutual bond of complicity, delightfully satisfied and entirely uncognizant that there were other wills rampant all around us. Jeremy and I were cloaked in our own ecstatic emanation of some how, by pure chance, it seemed to us, we assumed, succeeded with limpid ease in bringing about such a wonderous conclusion, as we saw it then. A sunset could not have been so golden to us.

We carried our bottles as covertly as we could—picture this, the three of us nonchalantly walking one behind the other in a column, each carrying four bottles of moonshine, two in each hand, in broad daylight through a corral full of horses, our ringing rowels sounding like a chorus of dinner bells—into the old barn, the one that has been ignored for years, for a forgotten reason, and left as a reminder of a time even I didn't know, but of which I only had half heard and hardly understood. For some reason and certainly not a valid one, the barn has been conveniently overlooked as though a curse would attend whoever had sense enough to demolish the poor thing— strangely, it seemed to die from an instant loneliness when it was abandoned. You see it today as only a disintegrating hulk, its huge, hand-squared logs rotten with open wounds bleeding ants, its plank roof splintered like a wooden ship against rocks, and now only used by wrens and sparrows and cats who religiously have their kittens under what remains of the board floor that even porcupines will not eat. It has been so forsaken for so long that it no longer has that metallic and familiar and masculine odor of horses. We carried the bottles, by this time our clinched fingers burning with fatigue, Lefty leading us, him now our acknowledged leader, which common sense would have loudly denied, up the ladder to the hayloft, where he carefully lifted away the hay until he uncovered beneath the hay in Uncle Pate's barn a hoard of similar bottles arrayed methodically and majestically in neat rows like soldiers on parade. We secreted our bottles with the others under the hay with a genuine kindness toward them, covered them with the dusty hay, and stealthily departed like darkened ships slipping past sentries.

"What now?" Jeremy asked.

"Nuthin, now. Ya jist leave everthin' ta me," Lefty said.

"We goin' ta git more?" Jeremy asked.

"We gotta 'nough for everthin' we got in mind," Lefty said.

"What's that?" I asked.

Lefty looked down at me as though I might have broken out with something for some time before he answered. "Don't ya try ta bullshit me, Dennis; ya got jist as much an idee as ya need ta have 'bout what we need."

"How much we gonna git?" Jeremy asked.

"I said I'd take care a everthin' and that includes 'how much,'" Lefty said.

"Ya said we'd split, didn't ya?" Jeremy asked.

"I didn't say that, but that's the deal."

It couldn't have been any other way, only Jeremy and I didn't know that then. That was something we had to finally understand for ourselves afterward. We then were still under the opinion that it was us who were using and Lefty only was a miracle, even if we had dumbly conceded his leadership.

"Go on and don't come back here," he said.

That night without a word between us, so twinlike in our thoughts were we, both were driven by the same lust, Jeremy and I dressed and left the house and went back to the barn and with only the silver spokes of the rolling moon around us, we painstakingly removed in feathery layers the dry and weightless hay from around the bottles.

"Forty-eight," Jeremy whispered, his voice like the footfall of a mouse across a cupboard.

"That's ninety-six dollars," I said.

"Hell, yes, that's ninety-six dollars," Jeremy answered.

We could not have been more overcome than had we found a chest of golden doubloons in Roaring Fork Creek. Neither of us had ever seen so much money, certainly not at one time, much less spread over any number of years, which we tried to silently remember. The sum was incalculable. We might as well had attempted to visualize the universe.

"How'll we split?" I asked.

"Three ways, Goddamnit," Jeremy said.

"He got most of it."

"He said we'd split, and that's what it means if there's three of us—three ways, Goddamnit."

"That'd be thirty-two dollars apiece."

"Son-of-a-bitch," Jeremy said.

"What can we do with thirty-two dollars?"

"Hell, I don't know. Anythin' we want, I guess."

"Jesuschrist."

It was a desperate thing to have to consider, particularly since neither of us had even imagined having thirty-two dollars to do with what we wanted, much less ever actually had it. Neither of us knew what thirty-two dollars could purchase. We had no experience with such a patrimony nor had we any reason to ever bother to think of what such a sum of money could purchase, since we had not ever done much more than bought one-cent candy or a Coca-Cola or a nickel handkerchief and later a cotton shirt or a felt hat with money that we had called our own money—money we thought we had virtually slaved for by milking cows, shoveling manure out of barns, collecting hens' eggs, or chopping wood, and, later, finally, scatter-raking and then learning to stack hay and set fence posts and, maybe, if something unimaginable happened, some ironic or fantastic incident occurred—luck—riding the backcountry to count cows like real cow-boys. Everything else we had ever needed had been either made by our mothers or sisters or bought in either Douglas or Casper by our fathers, and those were practical necessities. We could not even con-jure a single fantasy purchase just for the sake of purchasing, a frill, a folly, or an amusement. Even though we tried to imagine the things of which we had heard cowboys and other older boys talk—anything silly was both daring and acutely impressive to Jeremy and I then—we were unable to form substantial visions. We were completely igno-rant of the intricacies and glories of either having or using money, and, consequently, blissfully naive, which allowed us a great arena of thought devoid of any stringent and sobering realities. Our thoughts were chimeras, ethereal and dustily rosy and just as real as stories told in front of winter evening fires.

The next day Jeremy asked Lefty, "How are we gonna git the stuff there?"

"*We* ain't gonna. I am. You pups stay away from that barn. Ya'll damn lucky yer uncle didn't catch ya sneakin' out last night and queer the whole damn thing. I told you pups I'd take care of ever-thin', and I will, but I cain't do it with the two of ya pokin' 'round gittin' in the way."

"How'd ya know we was there?" Jeremy asked.

"Ya leave more tracks than a milk cow."

We fretted the days, and there were only two of them. If there had been more than two, we probably would have had nerve spells.

The morning was like a sapphire, mystical and poignantly vir-tuous, when Jeremy and I in heavy coats struggled onto the bed of the truck with Lefty. Uncle Pate and Tom sat in the cab, of course. The three of us ignored each other, not from any sense of secrecy or guilt or complicity, but because there still was the caste difference between us, one that neither Jeremy nor I could suggest to breach even in our new and wonderful relationship with him, and one that Lefty would chivalrously honor as a matter of the code, and which was not as easy as it may sound since the hay was pushed against the cab of the truck and all of us had to nestle in the hay otherwise we would we would have had to stop in Douglas either to have someone's bone set or fingers warmed. There really was no reason for us to speak to each other. As soon as Jeremy and I climbed onto the truck bed, we knew that the bottles had been boxed and that the boxes of bottles of moonshine lay under the hay and under a heavy, brown, musk-smelling tarpaulin that was always carried in the back of the truck on trips for riders to crawl under in case it rained.

Three

"We gotta right," Jeremy said. He looked as though he had been consigned to an eternity of pain, and he sounded like two rocks scraped against one another. With his hands planted firmly against his slim hips he looked like a tall and thin ewer with delicate handles.

"You pups ain't got nuthin'," Lefty said.

"Me and Denny got ever' right to know what we're gonna do," Jeremy said. "I thought ya said we were gonna split and be partners."

"We gonna split, but this here partnership ya keep spoutin' on about don't include no nursemaidin' you two. You two ain't got no idea what ta do with the stuff, so ya jist keep yer trap closed and I'll do the thinkin' and the doin' fer us," Lefty said. All the time he was talking to Jeremy he was looking up and down the street as though he were momentarily expecting something to appear wonderously in the middle of the street. "An' keep yer trap shut. Yer attractin' too much attention with yer whinin'. Keep still like Denny, here."

Both of them looked at me when he said that. I was standing next to the truck which we had parked in front of the Hotel Hemming watching—no, not watching, but staring at—the green and white window awnings marshaled in three neat rows above us, mesmerized by the symmetry of them, methodical and punctilious, and yet refreshing and refined.

"I don't know why I have to keep quiet; there ain't nobody paying' any attention to us," Jeremy said.

"Yer in the big city, now, pup; there's folks here who ain't all that friendly," Lefty said, his voice still flowing like molasses, slowly and voluptuously.

"Who'd pay any attention to us?" Jeremy asked, looking both up and down the street, suddenly searching for someone, but not having any more idea than I who might be interested in anything that we might say or do, for that matter, but now immediately involved in the implied threat, looking like he expected whomever to materialize beside us instantly. His voice even had assumed an innovative solemnity and his hands had slipped to his sides so that now he looked only like a knobby pole.

"That's why I'm here," Lefty said.

"Why?" Jeremy asked.

"Damnit, 'cause ya don't know a damn thing, Jere, and 'cause I do," Lefty said.

"I can take care of myself," Jeremy said.

"Shore ya can," Lefty said.

"Well, I can," Jeremy answered.

When no one bothered to answer him, he began again to look up and down the street. Across one street was the Gladstone Hotel and across another was the Townsend Hotel, both of them similar to the Hemming with the exception of the striped window awnings and I was glad to see that Uncle Pate had chosen the hotel with the green and white awnings, which gave to both Uncle Pate and the Hemming a certain class that I assumed both somehow deserved from the other.

Uncle Pate looked as though he just had posed for a formal portrait, an appearance that Jeremy and I had not ever witnessed, much less considered. After the faltering moment of recognition, he was an object of oblique scrutiny for us, and Tom, whom we were relieved to notice had not changed in appearance, came out of the hotel, Uncle

Pate said, "Take the boys around and show 'em the sights, but not too damn many sights, and be at the pens in the morning."

Tom laughed aloud.

"Don't worry, Boss, I know what to do," Lefty said.

"I know you know what to do. I don't want the boys to find out what to do just yet, and you know what I mean, Lefty," Uncle Pate said.

Tom laughed aloud again, and this time he turned his back on us, but I could see his shoulders shaking because I looked at him at the same time that Uncle Pate looked at him, but by the time Uncle Pate looked back at us, I already had my eyes adhered to him. Both Jeremy and I supposed we knew the things about which Tom was laughing, but we did not think for a moment that any of the grown men had the least inclination to suspect our knowledge of such things, and so we both did not smile, and we both tried to appear as incredulous as we could by looking at Uncle Pate directly and not even curiously glancing at Tom.

"I know what ya mean, Boss," Lefty answered, looking up the street as if carefully comparing hotel marquees.

"Good. See that nothing happens to them that Winnie wouldn't want to hear," Uncle Pate said, looking up the street the way he looked for cattle across a park, ignoring both Lefty and Tom and us. He had said what he had to say.

"Where'll we sleep?" Jeremy asked.

"In the truck," Uncle Pate answered.

"Oh," Jeremy said, disappointment coming suddenly over him.

Uncle Pate pulled his billfold from his coat pocket and thumbed over the sheaf of bills, and finally, with an uninterrupted meticulousness, he took four one-dollar bills out of his billfold and handed two each to Jeremy and I. "That'll be enough for you two," he said.

"Sure, that's 'nough. We're jist goin' ta the movie house," Jeremy said, flinging his thumb over his shoulder at the America Theater across the street.

"Hell, yes you are," Uncle Pate said. "C'mon, Tom; we have to meet those gentlemen," he said, and he and Tom, who looked back at Lefty for just an instant, went back into the hotel leaving us with the lie. That's what it was. A lie. Only Uncle Pate knew it a was a lie, even if both Jeremy and I were not really sure whether or not it was a lie, although we certainly suspected it was. Jeremy did not want to lie to Uncle Pate and to tell Uncle Pate that we were going to the movie house was only a ploy, a stalling action, and, consequently, in Jeremy's mind not really a lie just yet. Even if Uncle Pate knew it was a lie from the beginning, we didn't consider it one until we actually knew what we were going to do, and Lefty had not told us yet what we were going to do. Lefty did not answer at all concerning the movie house, so he was still as much an innocent as was still possible for any of us to be.

"All right, Lefty, what now?" Jeremy asked. "look's like yer goin' ta be nursemaidin' us whether ya want to or not, don't it," Jeremy said, looking as though he just found something very bitter in his mouth and was defying the aftertaste.

Lefty looked at Jeremy for a solid moment before he said, "Well, I'm goin' to git a haircut and shave and have myself a bath," he said, walking away from us, his bowed legs giving him the appearance from behind of a bowling pin that had been hit but not very hard. We followed behind him closely, into the wind that flowed as steadily as a river, not just because he was our fortune—we knew that, even if Jeremy wanted to argue with him about it—but also because we didn't know what else to do. Uncle Pate had been very clear that Lefty was to be our guide and guardian, and Lefty's responsibility to Uncle Pate for our welfare also entailed our responsibility to allow him to be whatever Uncle Pate wanted him to be to us. We were not yet so callous in our disregard of authority to confront either Uncle Pate or Lefty in such a situation.

"A bath?" Jeremy repeated.

"Yup," Lefty said to us.

"Why?" Jeremy said. "Didn't ya take a bath last night before we left?"

"Yup."

"Then why now?"

"Ya'll find out in a little while, Mister Smarty."

We followed Lefty up the street away from the hotels and suddenly we were in another part of town where there were roustabouts and drillers, used and ragged; sheepherders, muskily unwholesome as though they had worn something loathsome; and cowboys, graceless on the sidewalks, all of which both Jeremy and I had seen before all our lives, and other men who looked like what we thought hobos looked like, sallow and lethargic like they had just crawled off a freight train, shaggy men with unoccupied eyes; and clerks and businessmen, pallid and brisk, as each had something important but separate to do. Right there in front of us were five bars and Jeremy and I stood on the sidewalk and mouthed their names—Grand Central, Wyoming, Arcade, American, and Wonder Bar—hypnotically and artlessly, as though we had been instructed to memorize them, more bars than we had ever been allowed to see at one time. Up until this moment, we had never been introduced to such a staggering mass of obvious iniquity, and it took us an inordinate amount of time for the concept to form into a substantiality.

"You pups follow me," Lefty said, and he crossed the street, not even looking back at the restless horde of men, which Jeremy and I could not help but watch as they milled to and fro between the bars like apparitions, obscure and idiomatic to us, dim in the charcoal shadows of the doorways below the lambent masonry. We managed to follow Lefty until he said, "Ya can wait here and watch all ya want, but don't go anywheres."

When Lefty went into the barbershop Jeremy and I sat down on the curb.

"What if Uncle Pate saw us here watching?" I asked.

"He won't. He ain't never come to a place like this, you can bet.

Winnibeth'd skin him, if he ever did," Jeremy said, his voice full of righteousness as though he suddenly discovered a secret and was sharing it for the first time. Jeremy sounded like he were sparring with the lie itself, attempting to keep it at bay by insinuating a deprecation, a form of self-defense that is in itself only a delusion, but a perfectly natural way of retaliation against an oppression. The lie itself was a tangible, an odor that shrouds like wood smoke, and the guilt already had sifted like a fine lint over us and had become undeniable. The magnitude of the lie we already knew because we were not going to return or retrace any of our steps but were going to continue, stumbling forward like the soldiers of a diseased and defeated army. Although neither of us ever spoke of the lie, we both could feel it like a stomachache. When Lefty came out he looked like an oiled horse, and he smelled sweetly metallic like gasoline.

Even Jeremy did not bother to ask any questions of him. When he came out of the barbershop, he nodded, and we stood and followed behind him as he crossed the street, and then we were among the multitude and smelled all of them together, heavy and wet and musky. Lefty walked into the Grand Central Bar with us right behind him.

"You jist stick close ta me and nobody'll roust ya," he said.

He, Jeremy, and I walked the length of the crowded bar, acetous and mucid under an overcast of cigar smoke, jostled through groups of careless men, and waded through a continuous croon of the sounds of voices and glasses. Then we walked into a large room, lucent and yet illusory, where there were men playing cards and others standing and playing games—of which Jeremy and I had only heard descriptions—at brilliantly green tables.

Lefty stopped at a long table around which it seemed there were all the men we had been watching and contemplating. "I'm goin' ta play a little pan. You pups jist stand here and keep yer traps shut. 'N' don't stand behind me." He paused and looked us over like he were evaluating a horse's capabilities before he placed a bet on it. "It ain't polite ta stand behind a feller when he's a playin'," he said, and with that he pulled out a chair and sat down and ignored us, leaving us standing in the din of the voices and noises at the tables, as though this were the most commonplace of events, which it wasn't, at least not for Jeremy and I. Lefty knew we would stand there all night if necessary, simply because we had no idea of what else we possibly could do, and, certainly, we had no inkling of where we could go, now that we had committed ourselves to both him and the lie.

Stunned and enraptured with our new surroundings, we watched, silently and unmovingly as though we had been overwhelmed by an instant freeze, and yet as eagerly as though we were waiting our turn to run a race. We observed with intense fascination Lefty buying his white chips with two silver dollars and set the seemingly carelessly counted chips neatly in front of himself, leaving one of his large hands curled around them like a barricade, his pointed knuckles jutting forward aggressively like a bastion. The dealer, who looked like a loaf of unbaked bread with a white shirt and green visor, dealt the cards right to left from a package of several decks placed in the center of the table. It was easy for us to see how most of the game was played because it wasn't much different from a gin rummy game that sometimes the cowboys played in the bunkhouse when they didn't play poker. Sometimes we would get to play with them, carefully, of course, secretly among agreeable company, because neither Jeremy or I ever had any money, our reward for our work being the pleasure derived from fixing fence, shoveling manure, and raking hay for Uncle Pate. But it took us a long time to realize that some of the cards from the decks were missing, and so we began to count the cards we could see when one of the players put his cards face up on the table and we finally discovered that there were no eights, nines, or tens in the decks, which didn't make any sense to us then and still doesn't to me today.

When Lefty cashed in his chips—we couldn't see how many silver dollars he had won, although we tried as inconspicuously as we could to see—he stood up and with a slight brush of his hand he gestured for us to remain where we had been for the past hour, and he walked away through the tables and men and then he stopped and talked a long time to a man whom we had not seen before, a hobo we thought, a man who looked like he had a lemon in his mouth. He was wearing a dark blue pinstriped suit that was too long for him, which made him look shaggy.

Finally, Lefty motioned for us to follow him and the other man, and we immediately responded to his gesture as though we both had been leaning against an invisible barrier that suddenly had given way, so stationary had we kept ourselves. Lefty and the other man paused at a door and waited for us and then we all stepped outside into an alley, and the other man, who had not bothered to change his expression at all, said, "Who the hell are these kids?" He sounded as though he perpetually had a rash that irritated him.

"Ya don't have ta worry 'bout them, Charlie," Lefty answered.

"The hell I don't. What'dya bring a couple a kids for?"

Lefty looked at Charlie the same way he had looked at us, like he was evaluating a chance of some kind, for a moment before he answered, "Them's Pate's kin."

Charlie examined us, then. His face was shaped like a spade and he had excited blue eyes that flitted over us and everyone else and everything else, and his body was like the spade's handle. "Jesus Christ Almighty, Lefty, what the hell you tryin' to do ta me? That Goddamned old man'll kill both of us fer gittin' these two damn kids in on this deal."

"We can take care of ourselves," Jeremy said, as if he had been ordained to say things in a way that always seemed to irk someone, the same way he had spoken to Lefty that day at the fence, like two metal things being rubbed against one another.

"Piss on you, beanpole," Charlie said.

"Don't talk thet way to 'em, Charlie. They ain't spose ta hear thet kind a language," Lefty said.

"Holy shit, Lefty. You lost yer Goddamn mind bringin' them 'long."

"Ya jist leave it ta me, Charlie. I'm spose ta look out fer 'em, 'n' I reckon I can do 'er," Lefty said.

"I spose yer gonna look out for 'em down ta Mary's, too, huh?" Charlie snickered, and when he smiled his teeth were brown like leather.

"Ya jist leave 'em ta me, Charlie. 'Leven?"

"Sure, Lefty. 'Leven'll be fine. Ya just have the stuff there," Charlie said. He put a cigarette in his mouth and lit it with a match that could have come from his sleeve as far as we were concerned and tossed the match away.

"Don't ya worry none, Charlie," Lefty said.

Charlie turned and walked down the alley, but then he turned around and he looked right at Jeremy and said, "I don't like you, beanpole. Yer yaps too damn big fer yer own good," and then he looked at me and said, "I don't like you, either, Squatty. Ya don't talk enough, and ya watch too damn much fer yer own damn good." He looked back at Lefty and said, "Shit," and he walked away, hands shoved down into his pants pockets, rollingly as though he were on a deck and as if he might begin to whistle any moment.

"Why'd ya tell him we was Pate's kin?" Jeremy asked.

Lefty looked at Jeremy, this time like he also thought Jeremy talked too much, and he said, "So he wouldn't kill ya."

"What the hell does that mean?" Jeremy asked.

"It lets 'im know he could git himself hung if he wanted to," Lefty said, and he also turned and walked away down the alley, casually, as though nothing out of the ordinary had happened to us that afternoon.

Jeremy looked down at me and finally said, "Squatty," like he had just tasted something sour.

"He called you 'beanpole,'" I said, not retaliating against him, but saying it for defense, and a poor one, but the only one I could think of at the time, unless I called him a loudmouth, which I had sense enough then not to do, and we both started after Lefty, Jeremy a step ahead of me, his long legs outdistancing me, making me half run to keep up with him.

"Squatty," he said, and he snorted like a buck in rut, so I said, "Beanpole," and Lefty who was standing at the end of the alley said, "You two knock it off. We ain't got time fer any of that business."

"Then what kind of business do we have time fer?" Jeremy asked. "When're we gonna make the deal and git the money?"

"Ya leave that ta me," Lefty said. "The deals made. We jist gotta wait a while, that's all."

"What's the deal?" Jeremy asked.

"I said ya leave that ta me, Jere; I been here 'fore, 'n' you ain't."

"We gotta right to know," Jeremy said, at least still including me, which he had to do, because he couldn't by himself accept the whole responsibility for what the both of us had done and consented to. The consequences for just one of us would have been too much for any one person, particularly either Jeremy or I, to stand, and even though we also never spoke openly of what could happen to us if Uncle Pate found out just what we had done and were going to do, we both certainly were aware of the figure of Uncle Pate hovering about us, watching us, and clinging to us like an aroma.

A fine and silty guilt had sifted down upon our shoulders, but not enough to make it occur to either of us to turn back from whatever we were going to do next.

Lefty took us to a diner on Center Street. We sat at a long counter and directly behind each stool, there was a slot machine. Immediately, both Jeremy and I saw that there was a distinct rhythm to eating at the diner. Between each mouthful, we—all of us in the diner—were expected to turn on our stools and play the slot machines. Lefty ordered a barbecue beef sandwich and a cup of coffee for each of us from a woman who looked drained of whatever it was that gave vibrancy to life, and then he put in front of Jeremy and I a small pile of nickels. Choosing one, he turned on his stool—we also chose a nickel from the pile and turned on our stools, imitating Lefty as best we could, although anyone could plainly see that we were neophytes, because where Lefty's movements were fluid and thoughtless, ours were jerky, and he put it in the slot and pulled the handle and watched the rollers spin. While he was waiting, he pointed to the diagram on the slot machine that listed all the ways in which a person could win more nickels. We understood this easily enough, so we gallantly followed Lefty's example, the primary difference between the three of us being that Lefty won five nickels, while Jeremy and I didn't win anything, and, consequently, were even more eager than ever before to plunge nickels into the machines, which, of course, was the object of having the slot machines there.

Lefty added his five nickels to the small pile on the counter and then he turned around while Jeremy and I played the slot machines.

When our dinners were set on the counter, Lefty said, "Ya can leave 'em, now, and eat."

Calculating our first encounter with real chance, Jeremy and I had been able to add two nickels to the pile. We were silently exuberant at having dared and won.

By then the faces of the buildings across the street had been splashed with gold and the windows hurled back at us rays, brilliant and gleaming like magic swords, and we ate quietly in a diffused light, softly luminescent.

After we had finished eating, Lefty smoked a cigarette and Jeremy and I played the slot machines until he had smudged the butt into the ashtray and said, "That's it, gamblers. Time ta go."

When we stepped outside into the twilight, he said, "Don't worry none, pups. I'm keepin' a tally on the expenditures and expenses, and when we get paid off, ya can pay me back, then."

"I was wondrin' why you was so generous, wasn't we, Squatty?"

"I guess it's fair," I said.

"So when're we gonna make all this money?" Jeremy asked.

"We're on 're way, pups," Lefty said, and he was already walking away.

Uncle Pate said, "Then, what?"

"I walked 'em through the Grand Central so they'd have somethin' ta tell the other boys back home," Lefty said.

"That all?" Uncle Pate asked him.

"Yip," he said.

"Did he gamble?" Uncle Pate asked us.

"Who?" Jeremy answered.

"You gambled in front of them," Uncle Pate said.

"Well, I jist gave 'em a glance at it, Boss," Lefty said. "It weren't nothin', jist a little pan, no hard stuff, no harm done to 'em."

"I can just see it," Uncle Pate said, looking like he smelled something repulsively malignant. "Well, I hope you lost, so they won't want to try it," Uncle Pate said, shrugging his shoulders, knowing that there was nothing he could either say or do to change it, or to explain to Winibeth, if he ever had to do that, a resignation to a natural phenomena.

"Didn't win a thing, Boss."

"Then what?"

"Then I took 'em to dinner."

"Where'd you eat dinner?" Uncle Pate asked.

"Barbeque," Lefty said.

"Jeremy, how many nickels did you lose?" Uncle Pate asked him.

"Nickels?" Jeremy questioned. Uncle Pate knew that when Jeremy replied with redundant and foolish questions he was lying. It was a trick that Jeremy used that had not ever worked, but he had not ever figured out another way to not admit to doing something that he thought he might get in trouble for doing, and when he did it he always looked at Uncle Pate earnestly as though he were seeing him naked in church and were too polite to remark on the occurrence.

"You know just what nickels I mean. The ones Lefty gave you and Denny to play the slot machines with. Jeremy and Dennis, both of you are fools if you think Lefty won't make you pay him back somehow for losing his nickels. Well, it's your business, not mine;

I have more sense than to take any nickels Lefty offers me, and I suppose it's time for you two to learn what borrowing means," he said. "Well, take the truck down to the pens and spend the night there. Tom and I'll walk down in the morning," Uncle Pate said, as though he had just completed reading a book and had summarized it, not only to his satisfaction, but to anyone else's, for all he cared.

"We'll do 'er, Boss," Lefty said.

"If you go anywhere, you leave these boys at the truck," Uncle Pate said.

Tom snorted like a horse not sure of a rope and turned away from us and stared impatiently up the street.

Uncle Pate's concept of Lefty was a realistic one. He knew that an instruction to Lefty to remain for a night with a truck in Casper was equally as foolhardy as borrowing nickels from him, and for him to have given Lefty a direct order and for Lefty to have disobeyed that command would have been as embarrassing for Uncle Pate as it would have been disconcerting to Lefty. Uncle Pate would not have insisted at all for Lefty to have broken honor with him, which would have been painful for both men; consequently, Uncle Pate allowed Lefty an exit if he should choose to leave, which all of us, Uncle Pate, Tom, Jeremy and I and, particularly, Lefty, knew he would do.

Uncle Pate just did not realize at that time how far into iniquity Jeremy and I together had foundered like a crewless ship, wallowing on a restlessly bounding tide. He still considered us to be gentlemen kin who would honor his intimated instruction that even if Lefty did not remain with the truck, we were to do so.

Actually, the three of us did not have any intention to leave the truck alone, no matter where it was.

When we drove away and left Uncle Pate and Tom in front of the Hotel Hemming, Lefty said, "We gotta make a slight detour."

"Where we goin'?" Jeremy asked.

"Goin' ta visit a nice woman," Lefty said.

"She yer girlfriend?" Jeremy asked. "I didn't know ya had a girlfriend."

"I don't," Lefty said.

"Then who is she?" Jeremy asked.

"She's jist a girl," Lefty said.

"She a sister or sumphin'?" Jeremy asked.

"Not hardly, I reckon," Lefty said.

"Then who is she?" Jeremy asked.

"Damnit, Jere, stop askin' all them questions," Lefty said. "Be like Denny and watch."

"Ya mean Squatty, here?" Jeremy said.

"I mean Denny," Lefty said.

"If she ain't yer girlfriend or a relative, what is she?" Jeremy asked.

"I told ya," he answered.

"A nice woman," Jeremy said.

"Ya jist remember that," Lefty said, and then he drove the truck into an alley behind a solid line of little frame houses that in the moonlight looked like they were in pain and had smeared themselves with ashes in some kind of a desperate healing rite. When he drove the truck into a yard behind one of them and stopped, he said, "Now, you boys remember to be gentlemen and make Ol' Pate proud that yer his kin and know how to talk to nice ladies."

"We know how to talk," Jeremy said.

"By God, you sure as hell do," Lefty said.

"What the hell does that mean?" Jeremy asked him.

"You kin start watchin' yer yap right now," Lefty said.

Jeremy didn't answer, which was a relief to me and I am sure, now, that it also was solace for Lefty. The tone of his voice had become like that of a man who couldn't seem to hone a razor sharp enough.

Lefty got out of the truck and Jeremy and I went out the other door and Lefty said, "Shut the door. Don't slam it."

"We supposed to be quiet?" Jeremy whispered.

"She don't like loud noises. Try ta remember that, Jere," Lefty said.

By then there was a woman standing in an open doorway of the bent, little shack, silhouetted in a yellowish aura, fragile and ineffective. Finally she said, "Lefty? It's you, ain't it." She sounded like she had just set down a book and couldn't quite recognize reality.

"Shore, Mary, it's me," Lefty said. "Ya ain't had time ta forgit me."

"I ain't likely to, either. What the hell you doin' with that there truck in my yard?"

"Jist settin' her here for a spell, Mary; ain't nothin' ta worry 'bout."

"Hell there ain't. With you there's always somethin' ta worry 'bout."

"Thought ya said she's a nice woman," Jeremy said.

"You kin keep yer trap shut," Lefty said.

"She done swore," Jeremy said.

"Ever'body does," Lefty said.

"Who ya got with ya, Lefty?" she asked.

"Couple friends," he answered.

"Nice women don't swear none," Jeremy said.

"Shut up, Jere," Lefty said.

"They look like kids ta me," she said.

"Yip; they's jist kids," Lefty said.

"What the hell ya bring a couple a kids here for, Lefty?" she asked.

"Well, I didn't bring 'em for you-know-what, so don't even think about it, Mary," Lefty said.

By then we were standing at the back door with the light in our eyes but we could see her face. She looked as though she were bereaved. The corners of her mouth drooped sadly even when she spoke, and her eyes were like gray marbles. She leaned against the doorjamb so that she appeared to have taken on the aspect of the shack itself or that she and the shack had lived together for so long that the shack finally had become like her. She had no age; she and the shack were ageless.

"Listen, damnit, I got a niece here with me, and I don't want no Goddamn foolin' around with her by these two squirts," she said. "Peggy's a sweet girl, and I don't want her spoiled by jist anyone, you hear me?"

"They don't know what yer talkin' 'bout, that's how safe yer niece is."

"You ain't lyin'?"

"I ain't lyin'. Lemme in," Lefty said to her, and turning and looking at us standing just behind him, he said, "You two stay here a while. Don't do nuthin'."

"They kin come in, Lefty," she said.

"Not yet they cain't," he said.

"We ain't gonna do nothin' yet, Lefty, so they kin come in if they want," she said.

"We'll just wait here a while, Ma'am," I said.

"Listen ta that, will ya? He talks like a real gentleman, don't he? What's yer name, Sonny?" she asked. She bent forward as if that might help me to speak back to her, and even though her face was covered with shadow, I could see that her smile was no more than a sickle of moon.

"Dennis, Ma'am," I said.

"And what's yer name?" she asked Jeremy.

"Jeremy, Ma'am," he answered.

She stood up and still looking at us as though we were circus material, she said, "Ain't they sweet, Lefty."

"Sure," Lefty said.

"But I still don't want 'em 'round Peggy," she said, walking away from the door and into the room behind it where she became real, evolved into a person, although she still seemed to be fragile like a china cup. Lefty opened the screen door, glanced back at us briefly without saying anything, closed it and a moment later we heard her exclaim loudly, "No, damnit, not now," and then we couldn't hear anymore.

"You know what she is?" I asked Jeremy.

"A nice woman, I guess, like Lefty said, but she sure does swear, don't she?" he said.

"She's a prostitute," I said.

Jeremy stared at me as though I had committed a sacrilege for which I would not ever be able to atone. His mouth was as wide open as a cup, and he couldn't think of anything to say to help me repent.

"We're on the Sandbar," I said.

"Lefty's gonna kill you," he said.

"He isn't gonna kill me because he can't tell anyone we were here," I said. "Uncle Pate'd hang him if he found out where he took us tonight."

Jeremy digested this slowly but accurately. "Yer right, fer once," he said, and both of us felt the warm wrap of safety about our shoulders, a feeling that neither of us had really felt since the lie was told to Uncle Pate in front of the Hotel Hemming that afternoon. "How'd you know where we are?" he asked, as though something incredulous had just happened to him, something for which there could not be a reasonable answer.

"'Cause it's just like we heard it was, Jeremy; these here shacks lined up like little hats are the cribs where the whores live."

Jeremy turned and looked at the skyline, examined it, then looked up and down the long row of shacks. "By Goddamn, Squatty, yer right," he said.

"Thought you didn't swear," Peggy said.

She was standing behind us next to the truck. We couldn't see her well in the darkness, but her voice seemed resonant, like she was talking inside something.

"Who're you?" Jeremy asked.

"Who'd ya think I am?"

"Peggy," I answered.

She didn't say anything. Then she said, "Yer right about Aunt Mary; she's a whore like all these girls here."

"Oh, shit," Jeremy said, and he nudged me in the side with his pointed elbow, and he said, "What're we gonna do?"

"Ain't you never seen a whore before?" Peggy asked him.

"'Course not," Jeremy said.

"You ain't from here," she said.

"Why're you here?" I asked.

"Ma got 'rested," Peggy said.

"Fer what?" I asked.

"Whorin' like Aunt Mary. They'll let her go in a day. They always do," Peggy said. "They'll let 'em all go a day or two after they 'rest 'em. Ol' Jessen he just 'rests 'em and then puts 'em all back ta work. Ma and Aunt Mary been 'rested 'fore."

"Who's Jessen?" I asked.

"Mayor Jessen," she said.

"Why does he do that?" I asked.

"It's called a 'cleanup.' Church people make him do it," she said.

"How old are you?" I asked.

"Fourteen," Peggy said.

The door behind us opened suddenly and Mary kicked the screen door open, too, and shoved her head outside and said, "I've been lookin' all over hell fer you, Peggy. I don't want you 'round these two. You come in here, now." Mary still looked like she had just returned from burying a close friend.

"I want ta stay out here," Peggy said.

"Like hell, girl. You git in here right now," Mary said. She suddenly had become animated, her hands shaking in front of her like butterflies, and her voice sounded like a factory whistle.

"I'll run," Peggy said. Her voice cracked like a bean pod breaking, sharp and brittle. The light from the shack made her face yellowish like a faded flower and her eyes were like shiny coins.

"Oh, now, Peggy, Sweety, don't do that. Don't run away again from Aunt Mary. You know how bad that makes Aunt Mary feel. You c'mon, Sweety," Mary pleaded.

"Just go git her," Lefty said from behind her.

"You shut up, Lefty," she said. "Now c'mon, Sweety."

"I want ta stay and talk ta Denny and Jeremy," Peggy said. "I mean it."

"Hell, let her stay," Lefty said. "It ain't gonna' hurt nothin' that ain't gonna be hurt soon, anyway."

"You damn well stay out of it. I owe my sister ta take care of her."

"Then do it," he said.

"I would if you'd leave us alone."

"I'm gonna have another," Lefty said, and he walked away.

"Now you c'mon inside, Peggy, Sweety. These two nice boys can come along, too, and the three of you youngsters kin talk all you want."

"We better go in," I said.

"Well, she can go to hell, 'cause I ain't," Peggy said, and she turned around and ran behind the truck.

"Damn, you, you little bitch!" Mary yelled.

"Aw, shut the damn door, and c'mon," Lefty said.

"You little bitch," Mary yelled again, and she slammed the door.

"I knew she'd go away," Peggy said. She walked from behind the truck and stood by the back end in the dark again, suddenly substantial and yet ethereal, again in the moonlight that made the yard and the three of us appear chalky.

"Uncle Pate'd kill us if we talked to him like that," Jeremy said.

"Aunt Mary'll git drunk and fergit all about it," Peggy said. "Her and Lefty'll hit the sheets pretty soon, you watch." She disappeared and then we heard her climbing into the back of the truck and both of us thought right way about the same thing and so we ran to the back of the truck and both scrambled in with her and threw ourselves against the hay and packed boxes. Peggy smelled like lilac, indolent and wistful.

She stared us with thoughts like gnats, and then she said, "What you got there?"

"Where?" Jeremy said.

"There in that there hay," she said.

"Nothin'," Jeremy said.

"Yer lyin' sure as hell, Jeremy," she said.

"Naw, I ain't," he said.

"What's he got, Denny?" she asked.

"It's Lefty's," I said.

"What is it?" she asked. She had the same tenacity for questioning as Jeremy.

Neither Jeremy nor I said anything, and so she crawled on her hands and knees over her dress to the hay between us and poked until she felt her way into a box and then she said, "Thoser' whiskey bottles. Yer moonshinin'. Yer bootleggers."

"It's Lefty," Jeremy said.

"Bullshit. It's all three of ya," she said.

"It's mostly Lefty," Jeremy said.

"What'er ya gonna do with 'em?" she asked.

"We don't know," I said.

She contemplated this with a patience that was saintly. "Ya brung it cheer ta sell, didn't ya?"

"I don't know," I said.

"I believe ya," she said. "I wouldn't believe anythin' Jeremy told me, but I believe you, Denny."

"Squatty alles tells the truth," Jeremy said.

"Why you call him 'Squatty'?" she asked.

"'Cause he is," Jeremy said.

"He heard it from someone else this afternoon," I said. "He isn't anything but a beanpole. That's what the fella called him."

"Ya are short, Denny," she said. "Ya wanna go see the dead men?"

"What?" Jeremy asked, as though suddenly confronted with a miracle.

"They ain't really dead. They're jist gonna be," she said.

"Why?" I asked.

"'Cause they drink pure alcohol. There's a couple passed out up the alley. We kin go stare at 'em," she said. "Ain't nice ta roll 'em, though."

"Let's go," Jeremy said. He already was sliding off the tail of the truck. "C'mon, Squatty."

"I ain't goin'," I said. Not that I wasn't as curious as Jeremy to see these people who were going to die, and not that I hadn't seen dead people before. However, to be able to see someone you knew was going to die was an experience I had not had, and I, like Jeremy, wanted to be able to see the differences between those whom you knew were not ever going to die, like Uncle Pate and Aunt Winibeth or Tom, and those who already were dead, like an old relative, Cousin Elvira, who had died the past winter and whose funeral Jeremy and I had attended in Douglas, although the two of us only had seen her twice before in our lives that we could remember, anyway. But I couldn't go because Lefty had told us to stay with the truck, and Uncle Pate also expected us to stay with the truck even if the truck were not quite where he thought it might be. I couldn't go because I already had done too much now to ever be forgiven, and at least staying with the truck was something I could do, particularly since I was well aware that my sinning was not yet completed. Staying with the truck was an atonement for the past and future at the same time, and denying myself the opportunity to go stare at a person who was going to die was at least that much more of a sacrifice to mollify the coming penalties for which I knew I would pay.

You see how silly rationalization can be?

"Ya ain't goin'?" Jeremy asked.

"Nope," I said.

"Ya ain't afraid," he said.

"Nope," I said.

"Let's go," he said, and he and Peggy left, him leaning over her like a tree over a flower, the two of them fading away, their footsteps in the gravel like the steady sound of a meat cutter.

I leaned back against the hay and instantly went to sleep. It was the sound of the car that awoke me automatically. Like the sound of an alarm clock, the sound of the car slowing to enter the alley, the change in the sound of the car, the difference between its sound and the sound of a passing car was the signal to wake me, an instinct that called to me, and the car with no headlights came up the alley, turned into the yard, and stopped right behind the truck. When Charlie got out of his car he dropped his cigarette on the ground and grinded it into the gravel with the heel of his shoe. Then he said, "Hi, Squatty. Where's yer pals, Beanpole and Lefty?"

"Lefty's inside. I don't know where Beanpole is," I said.

"No loss there, Squatty. Go up and knock on the door and tell yer pal Lefty I'm here," Charlie said.

But Lefty already was outside and Mary was walking behind him, calling, "Peggy! Peggy, Sweety, where are ya?"

"Jesus H. Christ," Charlie said.

"Been waitin' fer ya, Charlie; let's git 'er done," Lefty said.

"Quiet 'er down, Lefty, ya want tha' whole Goddamn town here," Charlie said.

"Where's my Peggy?" Mary asked me.

"I don't know," I said, which was the truth, at least, which I was glad to be able to tell her, since I couldn't tell Uncle Pate the truth.

"Jesus H. Christ," Lefty said.

"My God, where is she?" Mary asked, her voice taking on that quality of the factory whistle and once again her hands fluttering in front of her.

"C'mon, Denny, let's git the stuff," Lefty said, jumping into the back of the truck. "Where's Jere?" he asked.

"They went to look at some men," I said.

"What men?" Charlie asked.

"Where'd they go? Goddamn, if he breaks her cherry, Lefty, I'll kill the skinny little bastard," Mary said.

"Here, Denny, you shove 'em down ta Charlie; damn that Jere, if'un he 'uz here this wouldn't take a but a second," Lefty said. "Oh, Hell, Mary, Jere ain't agonna do nothin' to yer little Peggy-Sweety."

I took the box from Lefty and pushed it along the truck bed to the end of the truck where Charlie took it and carried it to the back-seat of his car, repeating all the time, "Jesus H. Christ," as though he had just learned the new name and didn't ever want to forget it. Mary, looking like a cloth hanging from a line being whipped by wind, stood at the back of the truck alternating between being a supplicant and an autocrat. "Oh, God, please, little Denny, tell Mary where Peggy and that skinny, little son-of-a-bitch went off to; Goddamn you, Lefty, he'd better not find his peter tonight with 'er, or so help me God, I'll kill 'im and you, too."

"Goddamnit, Mary, shut the hell up," Charlie finally said.

"You kin kiss my ass, Charlie," Mary said.

"Why not; every other son-of-a-bitch has," Charlie said.

"You son-of-a-bitch," she said.

"Let's jist git this stuff taken care of," Lefty said, scooping hay away from the boxes, sliding them to me where I pushed them along the truck bed to Charlie, who wasn't able to work quick enough to keep up with the two of us.

"Why the hell don't you do sumpthin' worthwhile and help carry these here boxes?" he said to Mary.

"Go to hell, Charlie; ya didn't have any Goddamn right to talk ta me that away," she said, "and ya kin carry yer own Goddamn boxes."

"Hell, yer a whore, ain't ya?" he answered her, and she reached up and hit him ineffectually on his shoulder, and he brushed her aside with his arm, not actually hitting her or even trying to hit her, but just defending himself from another punch, the way a person might brush at a whiny mosquito, not bothered enough just yet to become serious about hitting it.

"Watch it, Charlie," Lefty said.

"Hell, she ain't nothin' but a whore; let 'er be," Charlie said.

"I reckon ya heard me," Lefty said, and the two of them stood there in the moonlight, both with pale faces, one standing on the bed of the truck, the other standing in the darkness so that half of his body seemed erased. Finally, Charlie said, "Let's git this stuff unloaded, Galahad."

"Ya know how much Peggy means ta me, Denny; please tell me where she done went off with that son-of-a-bitch, please," Mary said. "Goddamnit, Lefty, if he breaks her cherry, I'll lose a hell of a lotta money, and it'll be yer damn fault."

When we finished, Lefty jumped down from the truck and said, "Money."

"I got yer damn money, Galahad," Charlie said. He handed Lefty a lot of money, which Lefty counted carefully in the moonlight. "Look's good, Charlie," he said.

"Like always," Charlie said.

After Charlie drove slowly away, I said, "You've done this before."

Lefty looked down at me and said, "And, now, so've you, Denny. I gotta notion ta give ya Jere's share, but that'd jist cause trouble 'tween the two of ya."

"I don't want his share," I said. "I don't know whether I want my share."

"I know how ya feel, Denny. If ya want me ta keep it fer ya, I will, until whenever ya say."

"Well, keep it for now," I said.

That also was the truth. I didn't know whether or not I wanted the money. I felt then that if I refused to take any of the money, I somehow would be able to make up for what I had done behind Uncle Pate's back and for lying to him. I still at that point did not realize that the acts—the dealing in the whiskey running with Old Man Boudreaux and Lefty, which I knew would disappoint Uncle

Pate, and telling the lie—had been dishonorable, and since I did not know just what I had done, I certainly did not have an inkling of how to atone for it. I still had all that to learn.

When Jeremy and Peggy came back I was waiting for them in the back of the truck.

Jeremy climbed up onto the truck bed. He was breathing shallowly, the way a person breathes when they no longer are afraid but still excited and wondering, and he whispered to me, "By God, Squatty, I'm goin' ta marry Peggy."

"I wish you'd stop calling me 'Squatty'; it's embarrassing," I said.

"Well, ya are; did ya hear what I said? I'm goin' ta marry Peggy," he repeated.

"I heard ya," I said. "What did the people look like?"

"I'm so in love with her, Squatty; she's the most beeutiful girl I ever seed," Jeremy said, the same way he'd talk about a horse he had seen. He was just being himself, suddenly infused with a concept that defied any reason and based entirely upon a flick of the mind. For him to want to marry Peggy was no different than his wanting to fight Lefty, and, anyway, marriage was not yet a signal thought in mind—I had not suspected that it was in Jeremy's mind, either, although both Jeremy and I knew boys and girls who had been married when they were no older than us, so I innocently ignored his intoxication.

"Honest to God, Squatty, I shore love her. I gotta take her away from this place. She's too beeutiful to wind up a whore, and she ain't, yit; she's jist as pure as snow."

"Stop calling me 'Squatty'; what'd the people look like?" I asked.

"What people?" he asked.

"Them people. The ones who're gonna die. What'd they look like?" I asked, this time looking at Peggy who was standing at the end of the truck, the moonlight flowing over her hair.

"They looked jist like they always do, kind of sickly; what're you two whisperin' 'bout?" she asked.

"What's the difference 'tween them and someone who's really dead?" I asked.

"People who jist died don't stink and these people do, kind of sour and like a dog at the same time," Peggy said.

I thought about what Peggy had said, but I had a hard time reconciling the images that came to my senses like raindrops. I finally said to Jeremy, "Have you told her?"

"What're you two whisperin' 'bout?" she asked again.

"I ain't sayin'," I answered, and I stood up out of the scattered hay and walked to the end of the truck bed and jumped down next to Peggy and smelled the luxurious lilac. Then I walked toward the shack, saying, "Mary's all heated you aren't home."

They were sitting in a yellow glow, the corners of which were gray and the room smelled of the same lilac as Peggy and cigarette smoke, vapidly and profusely burdensome. When Jeremy and Peggy and I finally came into the room, Mary stood up and pointed at Jeremy and said, "If you broke her cherry, I'll kill you."

"Oh, hell, Mary get off the kid. He ain't done nothin' ta her," Lefty said.

"How the hell would you know?" she said, and then she rushed at Peggy who was standing as still as a vase flower, wan and small. Reaching out to her as though she had seen something wonderful and unknown about her, she whined, "Are ya all right, Sweety? Did the little bastard do anything to ya?"

"He ain't done nothin', Aunt Mary; he ain't got sense ta," she said.

"Thank the Good Lord," Mary heaved.

"I wanta take Peggy home," Jeremy said.

"Good Christ Almighty," Lefty said.

"You ain't takin' my Peggy-Sweety anyplace, you little bastard," Mary said, finding a reservoir of strength enough to stand in front of Peggy and shield her from some terrible catastrophe that had emerged from a gray corner of the room.

"What?" Peggy asked, as incredulous as Lefty or me or Mary.

"She cain't live like this here; I want ta marry her," Jeremy said.

"Fergit it, pup; I ain't 'bout ta take ya back ta the Old Man with a little whore hangin' 'round yer neck," Lefty said.

"Just what the hell does that mean, Lefty? When ain't a whore good 'nough fer you, you son-of-a-bitch?" Mary said.

"I ain't the one who figures he wants ta git married, for Christ's sake," Lefty said.

"I ain't a whore, yit," Peggy said.

"Yer close 'nough," Lefty said.

"Well, I ain't 'bout ta let 'er go, anyhow," Mary said.

"Hell, no, you ain't; jist remember how much money she's worth ta ya the way she is," Lefty said.

"You damn right I remember. Anyhow, I got a responsibility for her 'til my sister gets out, and I gotta remember that, too," Mary said.

"I ain't goin', anyhow," Peggy said. "I told ya he 'uz short on sense. I wanta be a whore."

"How can ya say that?" Jeremy said. "I love ya."

"I don't love you," she said, "and I ain't goin' nowhere with ya."

"Holy shit," Lefty said.

"I've had 'nough talk like this here," Mary said. "Goddamn you, Lefty, ever' time ya show up 'round here ya do somethin' like this. Jist ya don't come 'round here no more."

"This ain't my fault, Mary. I ain't the one wallerin' in goo, so ya jist take it easy, now. Jere, ya damn fool," Lefty said.

"I mean it, Lefty. You're a sweet bastard, but I'm just plain sick of ever'thin' that happens when you come 'round here. I don't know why in hell ya done brought a couple of wet-behind-the-ears kids, anyway," Mary said.

"I ain't wet-behind-the-ears," Jeremy said. "I thought ya loved me," he said over Mary's head to Peggy who was standing behind her aunt peering at Jeremy, who was standing on his tiptoes, which he didn't at all have to do.

"Shit," Peggy said.

"Then why'd ya hold my hand?" he asked.

"What'd ya hold his hand for?" Mary asked. She turned her face sideways, but was still defending Peggy against an imminent attack from Jeremy with her body. "What else did ya hold?"

"Nothin', damnit, Aunt Mary," Peggy said.

She turned around and looked at Jeremy who looked as though he had just been bitten by his dog. "What the hell did you hold of hers?" she asked.

"Hold?" Jeremy repeated.

"You know what I mean," she said.

"He ain't got an idee what ya mean, Mary," Lefty said. "C'mon, pups, we're aheadin' out."

"And don't come back, Lefty; you're a mistake, and I don't want you or any of your kids around here again," Mary said.

"I ain't leavin,'" Jeremy said.

"The hell you ain't, kid," Mary said.

Lefty didn't even wait for Jeremy to answer Mary; he took Jeremy by his thin arm the way one takes a shovel handle to carry the tool to the next row. With no apparent effort, as though through will alone, he placed Jeremy on the wooden sidewalk in front of the shack the way one would set a stool in the middle of a floor. Before we made it to the corner Mary already had recovered enough from Lefty's departure—and yes, it was Lefty's departure, because neither Jeremy nor I yet had settled to a substantial thought, much less an understanding that we had actually exited, we had moved so quickly—to yell after us with the expiation of unregulated rage, "Lefty, Goddamn you, don't you ever come back here, 'specially with any Goddamn kids, you hear me?"

And Lefty with a fine expression of his inherent impudence gestured with his wrist the way one might brush away an irritating thought, the harsh finality of the movement stranding Mary better than would have a flood.

It was daylight when I awoke. The sky had been washed like a window. When I looked at Jeremy he also was awake, his eyes looking like they had not yet had the needed time to flood with the liquid beryl that made his eyes so blue, the freckles on his face ripening in the sun like seeds.

"You still in love, Beanpole?" I asked. It was not something that I had to ask him; it was not as though I had been induced by a hypnotic thought the night before to say that very thing upon awakening. I could have denied the pleasure of asking him that question that morning and all the rest of the summer, for that matter, but like so many things that had happened to both of us the past weeks and days, the temptation to ask him that question preceded any definite or formed thought, just like taking the whiskey and telling the lie, and now this, insulting the best friend I had, even if he was a cousin.

"Goddamn you, Squatty," he said, and from his wrapped-up and prone position, his long arm uncoiled and his skinny fist hit me in my face. That was a purgation for both of us; a relief for him from his embarrassment, and releasing for me of everything that had happened and had been said between us, and I fell on top of him and hit him, pounded a dozen little brown seeds that had been sprinkled on his face, hit him at least twice before his mind and body coordinated the realization that I had hit him and was going to hit him again. And then he yelped, just like a dog kicked by its master, and he grabbed me and rolled on top of me and flailed at me, his long arms jointed like a broken piece of Timothy-grass, angularly. I struck back at him, now furious and unseeing and wild and screaming, both of us yelling at the other, and both of us hitting the other but so flat-handedly that neither of us felt much of anything and probably could have continued doing that all day with neither of us actually hurting the other since no single blow besides the first ones were being aimed, only thrown uselessly like we were hitting at mosquitoes.

Then just as suddenly we both were standing on our feet to where we had been jerked and I was spinning off the back of the truck, toppling and falling to the ground, and just before I actually fell, I looked up to see Jeremy thrown like a bag of oats into the corner of the truck against the cab and Lefty standing in the middle of the truck bed, his huge fists clenched until his knuckles were strangely white. When I rolled over to my hands and knees and stood up, Lefty was looking at me, his face passive and unconcerned, like he was going to make a judgment concerning a strand of barbed wire, as though nothing important had ever happened or was ever going to. Jeremy was sitting, picking isolated pieces of dry hay from his clothes, not looking at Lefty and ignoring me, concentrating on the pieces of hay. I stood in the dust and knowing full well that I did not have the courage to challenge Lefty physically, I decided to confront him silently and sullenly, which is nothing more than a harmless retaliation, a defiance founded on shame, but I somehow had to demonstrate to myself some self-respect. So I stood there looking at him, feeling the blood running out of my nose, tasting the metallic blood in my mouth and knowing that it was dripping from my chin onto my shirt.

"We ain't got no time fer this kinda stuff," Lefty said. "We ain't outta here, yit, and till we are, we gotta be tagether. Ya'all kin fight the hell outta yerselves when we git back ta the ranch. Next one a ya takes a swing at tother gonna git one, an' I ain't kiddin'," he said. "Now, the two of ya git up and git cleaned up 'fore the Boss gits here and sees all this," he said, jumping down from the truck bed and walking past me as if I were a weed.

Then I looked at Jeremy and saw that he had dried blood on his lips, turning black and ragged, and I said, "I got ya." I was surprised; I had not had time to think that I would do something that would be visible, and seeing Jeremy with his blood on his lips was at the same time astounding, electrifying, and curious. If I had heard that I had done this to him it would have made no impression on me, but seeing that I had accomplished this, exposed his blood, without having thought about doing it to him was very moving and poignant.

"Yeah, well, I got you, too," Jeremy said.

We both heard Lefty say, "You two git up ta the trough and wash up. Boss'll be here pretty quick, and I don't wanta haf ta explain how the two of ya got blood all over yerselves."

Jeremy and I stood behind Uncle Pate and Tom, who stood at the edge of the platform looking down into a loading pen. Lefty stood behind us with other men, Henry Johnson of Medicine Bow, Thomas Crosswell of Kaycee, and Joseph Myers of Powder River and men that belonged to all of them, so that the platform was crowded and smelled tartly of leather. It appeared that everyone who was in Casper had come to see Uncle Pate's bull.

When we had walked across the platform to stand behind Uncle Pate, and when he had known we stopped behind him, he had turned and had looked at us and then examined us as if we might be a pair of bulls he had come to see, rather than the bull into which he already had invested his time and money. Then Tom had turned and had looked at us, me with my swollen and bluish nose and Jeremy with his bloated, purple lips, our clothes dusty, but, at least, with our hair combed and the dried blood washed away so that Jeremy's freckles could be counted. Neither Uncle Pate nor Tom condescended to look at Lefty, who did not look at them either, but looked at the new bull, as though there could be nothing more important to do than silently evaluate the qualities of the bull, who looked like he just stepped from a barbershop where his hair had been washed and curled and his horns manicured to look like washed agate and his hooves polished to look like a cleaned stove.

"We'll talk about it later," Uncle Pate.

"Yessir," I said.

"Christ," Tom said, snorting it like a horse would have done, surprising me that he hadn't pawed with his foot, too.

Then three other men walked across the platform and stood

near Lefty, two on one side, the other behind him, men with white, ambiguous faces like they were made of dough, but carved with angles and given obsidian eyes, one of the men wearing a dark blue pinstriped suit like Charlie's, only this man's suit fit him.

Uncle Pate turned around again and said, "What is it, Suitcase?"

"I got a message fer yer boy, here: Lefty," the man said, his voice sounding flat.

"Well?" Uncle Pate said.

"The message ain't fer you," Suitcase said. He didn't look at Lefty but looked right at Uncle Pate, both men looking at each other as though they each had heard a universal truth but hadn't decided yet to do anything about it.

"I'm the one who'll have to pay the price, so just say it, Suitcase," Uncle Pate said.

"Well, yer boy here ain't supposed to bring anymore stuff into town. The boys up town don't care fer the competition," Suitcase said.

"All right, Suitcase, you delivered the message," Uncle Pate said and he turned around.

"Let's go," Suitcase said, and he and the other two men walked away, but then he turned around and said, "Hey, Lefty, yer ol' pard Charlie ain't feelin' so well today. He had a lotta thinkin' to do last night, 'n he decided ta do business somewhere else, and ya can pass that along ta Boudreaux, too. Ya wanta pass along a condolence?"

"Maybe tamorry," Lefty said.

"Oh, yeah, nice bull ya got there," Suitcase said.

Uncle Pate turned around and looked right at Suitcase and said, "Yes, Suitcase, it's a nice bull I got there, and it's a nice bull I plan keep around a while, or I'm going to have a nice time hanging someone."

Suitcase shrugged and turned and walked away, the other two men falling in behind him as if they had been trained to march that way.

Four

The amber days of August came and went. The chokecherries were dark like obsidian and extravagantly saccharine. The forest smelled like dust, airless and venerable like a musty book, and the light fell in solemn, golden bars between the ferns, playing like dying heroes in the waning days of the summer.

Jeremy and I had scatter-raked meadows that looked like fields of buckskin until the rake tines finally lost their ancient rust to look like burnished swords.

Neither Jeremy nor I ever spoke of what had happened between us, like two enemy sentries held motionless by a truce neither understood but only recognized, tolerated, trying to distance ourselves from our pursuers, feeling this rather than actually knowing this, as if our minds had lost their ability to reason such an enormity. In our silence, our lives rumbled with reproach and a fine jonquil pollen of sin settled downward and over us until every day we wore guilt like iron.

We did not really see Lefty that season. Sometimes we would see a lone rider sitting at rest along the top of a distant ridge above a meadow, and we would know that it was Lefty, but that fleeting knowing was all we felt, a sense of distance, delicate and obscure.

Uncle Pate also was surrounded by a sense of shadow, remote and enigmatic, as though there were fingers kneading his mind for a certain thought, an idea as delicate as a flower. His silence was like thunder in our ears, as we watched him and Tom stand on the gingerbread porch together in the lambent evenings as the mountains took on an iron tint, the two of them joined together like two trunks from a single root and with all the elasticity of stone cairns.

Through the haying season all this flowed continuously like a river.

They finally came. Although neither Jeremy nor I had discerned what we had been waiting for, we had surmised that we had been waiting for something, the way a person yearns for a summer rain, not seeing the warning of Timothy-grass fluttering and then, suddenly finding oneself emersed and in the open. Lefty was the one who told Uncle Pate and Tom that they were coming. Jeremy and I heard his galloping horse—it sounded like dollops of thunder being sprinkled restlessly onto the road—and later Uncle Pate came to our bedroom in the darkness before dawn and said, "You can come along now."

We rode through a sapphire twilight with that quick, smooth trot of horses used to the mountains, different from the hesitant gait of horses raised in the flat country, sure and steady and constant, the sound of horses hooves stepping on rocks, the sound hollow as though we all were riding in a bucket. Uncle Pate led, followed by Tom and Lefty and Curly Jones, Henry Carter and Edward Curtis, and, finally, Jeremy and I, and our rifles, Winchesters passed out unceremoniously to us the way a person deals cards to players by Uncle Pate while Aunt Winibeth stood outside the office, a specter, unenduring now in white, repeating, "Pate, they only are boys," over and over, a tinsel sound like a taut wire, and Uncle Pate saying, "They still will be boys when they return, Winny, but not quite the same boys, that's all," the sound of his voice like a cathedral bell, heavy, thrilling, and ominous.

We could feel the ground under us, and knew that we were doing this because of what we had done, what we had manufactured between us and then with Lefty had consummated, and that this thing was finally the punishment from which we had tried so futilely to distance ourselves, and all the while we rode we could hear the whine of their car below us on the road, wheezing as it tried to climb over the ruts that grew in the road to the foot of Boudreaux's Draw where the road and even the ruts stopped abruptly.

We did not race them. We just rode like the riding itself was the mission and did not focus on what was going to happen at the end of the ride. When we finally dismounted in the trees and the horses were left with Jeremy and me, Tom looked back at us, the sun finally on his poised face and he said, "This time don't lose 'em."

"Nossir," Jeremy said.

Tom looked at me, and I answered, "Nossir." That seemed to satisfy him, and he turned and walked after Uncle Pate. We could hear below us the sound of things breaking, metal and glass things. Uncle Pate put up his hand and he sat down with his rifle across his knees, and the others stopped and stood, their rifles in their hands, except Lefty, who had a pistol in his hip pocket, and they all lounged in the still day, limpid yet from its dawning.

When the breaking at Old Man Boudreaux's still finally stopped, Jeremy and I could hear a single voice, as though that person were alone in an auditorium say, "If ya can still hear me, ya old bastard, the boys in town don't wantcha messin' in their business anymore."

Then Lefty walked down the hill, and Uncle Pate stood up and then Tom and the others followed slowly behind Lefty down the hill and out of our sight. Jeremy and I crawled to the top of the hill so we could see this part of what we were supposed to watch, a new scene in an old play, suddenly written by Jeremy and I who only recently had joined the cast, and who really had no right to have interjected ourselves into the tradition, the play that had been acted out for years before we ever had rode our first horse across Uncle Pate's ranch. Old Man Boudreaux was lying on his back surrounded by what had been his still, but now was just so much broken metal and glass and twisted copper wires, with blood on his face and on his white shirt, spattered as though someone carelessly had shaken a paint brush of blood at him. His gray hair was unruly and his arms were spread wide like a greeting to an old friend. Calvin was trying to crawl on his hands and knees and one of the men kept kicking at him, shoving him down with his foot, pushing Calvin to his stomach and then stepping on him to hold him still. But Calvin didn't have sense to stay still, and so it would begin again, and Calvin was saying "Oh, God. Oh, God," sounding like he had been surprised and couldn't think of anything else to say.

"I wouldn't do too much a thet," Lefty said, his voice like syrup flowing over the edge of a plate, as it always sounded, with unseemly monotony and the unvarying impudence he always carried with him.

Suitcase, with an axe handle in his hands, turned and looked up at Lefty. His mouth took on the aspect of just having discovered a new and pleasant taste, but his eyes were the same as we had seen them in Casper when he had stood on the platform, like agate, as though they were an inanimate part of him. He seemed as if he might move like a human but couldn't feel like a human, eyes like a large snake, opaquely vacant. Then he looked past Lefty and saw the rest of them, Uncle Pate, Tom and the others, spread in a line behind Lefty. Whatever he had in his mouth lost its sweetness and turned sour, and his voice sounded like a piñon nut being cracked when he said, "The hell with you, Lefty." He dropped the axe handle and his right hand went inside his dark blue pinstriped suit coat, and at that moment Lefty killed him with his pistol.

There was a terrible expanse of time between that snap of the pistol being fired and when Lefty looked back up the hill at Uncle Pate. I didn't know at the time why he looked at Uncle Pate; I could read nothing in his expression, but I saw Uncle Pate nod curtly at him, as though he were telling him it was all right for him to take a cookie from a jar before his supper. Lefty walked back up the hill past Uncle Pate and Tom and the others and by us, saying, "You pups take cere a yerselves," and to his horse and rode away.

Two days later Jeremy and I were in the barn moving hay when Uncle Pate came and sat down on a milking stool. Both Jeremy and I knew that this was the culmination of our experiment, that what was to follow now was what we had guaranteed an undisturbed title to, and that now there was nothing left for us to do—since we had done everything we set out to do—but stand or sit and receive whatever it was we were to own for the rest of our lives for having done what we had done. We were relieved that the moment had finally come, because we thought we needed to have everything explained to us, and then to acquire the recompense that we deserved.

With slow precision Uncle Pate pulled a cigar from his coat pocket and carefully lit it—something no one was allowed to do in the barn, but something he could do, because, after all, it was his barn, and he could do anything he wanted—and when the air smelled husky with the cigar smoke, and after he had carefully examined something near the toe of his boot, he said, "Well, Lefty was consistent and there always is a great truth to a man who is consistent, and Lefty was the most truthful man I have ever met. You can always count on a man who is truthful; there are no tricks to a man who is truthful. He was an honorable man, and that is the best anyone can say of another man. He had a great integrity about him, and I'm glad that the two of you had your association with him, and I hope you will remember him.

"Remember him kindly, because I will, and I will miss him, and I suspect that you two also will miss him.

"What happened was not really your fault even though you think that it was. It's all right for you to think that; thinking that will not hurt you, either now or in the future, just as long as you don't believe it."

"Will he ever come back?" I asked.

"No," Uncle Pate answered.

And, he didn't. Later, when I was grown, and I certainly was not grown then, you know I traveled a lot, and I always watched for an impudent walk and listened for a voice like syrup flowing, but I did not ever see Lefty again. You have to know a man's truth to be able to see how truthful he is. Lefty's truth was a little different than yours or mine, but he was, as Uncle Pate said, a truthful man. Now it's time for a piece of your mother's apple pie.

A Hoover Steak

SUDDENLY HE COULD SEE. HE COULD SEE THE DARK LOOM OF A HILL'S silhouette, like the long shadow of a ship at anchor. He could see the outline of Phyllis's face through her cigarette smoke. Her features looked gentle and gracious in the forming twilight.

He could smell her through the odor of her cigarette smoke. She smelled like a flower, luxurious and abundant. He rolled his window down, rested his elbow on the sill, and inhaled deeply of the frail air. He supposed they all smelled like whiskey, but he couldn't smell the whiskey, though he could still taste the hot sourness of it.

In the backseat, Eddie said, "Anyone want a swig?"

"Not any more. It'll be light pretty soon," Davey said.

"How about it, Sis?"

"You heard Davey, Eddie," Phyllis said, her voice haggard and scratchy, like someone walking slowly in sand. She violently ground out her cigarette in a glass ashtray she had brought from the cabin.

"Well, if no one minds, I think I'll have a swig," Eddie mumbled with a lazy arrogance.

"For Christ's sake, Eddie, don't get drunk," Phyllis said.

"Who cares? I don't have to hunt," he said.

"Well, I don't want my brother to be drunk when I shoot my deer," she said, turning her shoulders and looking at him. When he lit another cigarette, she could see his hair, the color of winter straw, tumbling like a wave from under his gray Scotch tam, and his dispassionate blue eyes watching her. She knew he was getting drunk and would flaunt his drunkenness and his indiscriminate insolence. With a snap of his wrist he extinguished the match, and the backseat of the Model T was dark again, but she could see the glow from his cigarette and the sharp line of his long nose and his razor-edge cheekbones. Ring, the big Irish setter, sat up next to Eddie and looked at Phyllis, and even if she couldn't see his eyes, she could see his pink tongue lolling out of his mouth and smell his husky breath, and she looked back at Eddie. She felt her chest quiver, and she turned back. "I wish you wouldn't get drunk," she said.

"I won't, Sis. How about it, Davey? Sure you don't want a swig?"

"Nope. Not a good idea now, Eddie," Davey said.

"Well, Ring, it looks like it's you and me," Eddie said.

"Oh, my God, Eddie, you won't give Ring any of that stuff?" Phyllis said.

"He won't drink it," Davey said. He looked at Phyllis. It was light enough now so he could discern her dark, shoulder length hair and the neat finger waves that flowed to the edge of her white forehead.

After a while, when the morning became purple as amethyst, Davey said, "Let's get out and be ready, Kiddo. They'll come along the side of the slope on their way down to the beaver dam."

He opened the door and stepped out. He was big and when he left the Model T it sighed.

Phyllis turned around and looked at Eddie, who slouched lawlessly, rubbing his hand over his face, his gaze moping somewhere near the floor, the Lucky Strike hanging pale from his lower lip. Phyllis sat starkly silent, watching him. Ring sat up and put his front paws on the back of the seat and panted at her, his breath warm, curdled, and a string of drool dripping on the seat. Finally, she turned and softly opened her door and stepped out, easing the door back into its place.

When Davey looked over the top of the black car, he could see plainly how white her face was, a seeming disparity between her face and her glossy hair, as if one or the other might not be real. She was wearing blue bib overalls and one of his white shirts, and he thought she looked as if she were wearing a tent over her shoulders and carelessly stuffed into her pants.

Davey opened the back door and took a rifle off the floor, being careful not to hit Eddie, who was limper than any physical law should have allowed. He closed the door and walked around the back of the car and stood behind Phyllis and smelled the exhilarating, pervading odor of her perfume. He leaned the rifle against the side of the car and put his hand on her shoulder. Under her shirt and fluid skin he could feel her muscles flowing like tight piano wires, and her arm stretched like a cat's.

"Now don't you get me excited, Davey," she purred.

"I won't," he said, not wanting to believe any word of what he said. He took his fingers away from her shoulder. "Here's the rifle," he said, picking it up by its stock.

She turned around, put out her hand, and took the gun with a determined movement that left no doubt of her purpose. "Let's get going," she said, looking up at him. His face was round and clean shaven, and his jaw was squared and blue in the twilight. It was light enough that she could see his almost gray eyes and flimsy eyebrows.

"Whoa," Davey said, the sound of his voice secretive and leisurely. "We don't have to be in any hurry, Kiddo. They'll be along, like I said."

He looked up through the trees, finally standing like individuals, having been singled out from each other by the dawn. "They'll come right along that slope. You just wait and see. C'mon," he said, taking her by the hand and leading her past the door where Eddie leaned like a slattern, and where Ring watched him as though he had religious significance. Davey also wore bib overalls, and strung across his waist was a gold chain. His shirt also was white, and he wore a gray felt hat tipped back on his broad, white forehead. Both Davey and Phyllis were wearing heavy leatherwork shoes like the ones Davey wore when he was in the engine. He led her to the hood of the car.

"Lean over the fender and rest the rifle just like I showed you," he said softly. Phyllis leaned her flat belly against the fender and rested her left elbow on the hood and pulled the stock into the hollow of her right shoulder.

"Good," Davey said. "How does it feel?"

"Fine."

"You can relax, now, and we'll just wait."

"Eddie's going to get drunk," she said, holding the rifle across her chest and looking up at Davey.

"He's all right. I don't mind."

"You haven't seen him like he's going to get. I know. I've seen him get this way before, and he gets tough. I can tell by looking at him."

"He's always been nice to me. I can handle him."

"Be careful with him, Davey. He gets crazy sometimes. Mean crazy."

"He'll be all right."

"Davey?" Phyllis said. Her voice sounded far away. "See?"

Across the draw and up in the dusky timber, three does had emerged like apparitions. They stood in a line, each with her ludicrous, huge ears turned toward Phyllis and Davey.

"Do it," Davey whispered.

Phyllis raised the rifle and rested her elbow on the hood and slipped the stock into her shoulder hollow just the way Davey had shown her, and she watched the doe in the lead. Time felt to her like it suddenly had paused for something momentous to happen. Convulsively, she jerked the trigger and the report thudded like an axe on wood.

She stood holding the rifle in her hands the way an eagle holds a rabbit in its talons, her mouth open and her eyes so wide Davey could see how white they were.

The doe folded up and crushed herself like an emptied egg.

"I did it! Oh, Davey, I did it!" Phyllis screamed, turning to Davey, who grabbed the rifle away from her and held it over his head.

"You got her, all right!"

Phyllis entangled him with her arms and shoved her head against his hard chest. "I did it," she said again and again.

"Let's go and dress her out," he said, laying the rifle across the hood. He took her arms away from him, and taking her hand, he led her down into the grass and ferns and across the draw. He could feel her hand clutching his, and when he started up the other side, she grabbed his arm with her other hand and dug her fingernails into his skin under his shirt, but he didn't say anything to her. He pulled her along behind him, as though he might be pulling a child on a sled.

When he reached the doe, he quickly turned her on her back with her head uphill. Reaching into his front pocket, he took a leather knife sheath out and in the same motion slipped the knife from its sheath.

"Hold her legs," he said.

When he bent over the doe with his knife, Phyllis gasped. "What are you going to do?"

"Gut her," he said.

"Yes, but—where are you going to cut her?" she asked, shrinking away and raising her hand to her throat, staring at him.

Davey stood up. "There," he said, pointing with the knife blade to her genitalia.

"Oh, no, you can't. You can't do that," she said with a stubborn bewilderment.

"That's the way you have to do it," he said, trying to sound gentle and patient.

Phyllis turned away. "I'm going back to the car," she said. "I can't watch you. I didn't know it had to be that way."

"I'm sorry." He watched her walk back down the slope through the trees, and he thought that even in bib overalls, she was pretty snappy looking.

When Phyllis climbed up the bank to the car, Eddie was sitting in the open door, his feet on the running board, a new cigarette hanging from his lower lip. His cap was slanted impudently across his forehead. His overalls were dirty with black bloodstains of yesterday's deer on them, and his white cotton shirt was grimy where sticky pine pitch and dirt had mixed. He hadn't shaved in two days and the dark film of beard made his face look like it hadn't been washed in a long time. "Goddamn thing's empty," he said, flinging the bottle away into the draw, where it clinked into the ferns. His breath smelled old and sour.

"Good. Now, maybe you won't get any drunker," Phyllis said.

"I'll damn well do what I want, Sis. I'm a big boy now, or ain't you noticed?"

"Yes, Eddie, I've noticed. You can do what you want. Just don't make any trouble with Davey, okay?" She almost reached and touched his arm, but she stopped herself and stood in front of him with her hands locked behind her.

Suddenly, he said, "Boo!" and he jumped up at her. She started to fall over backward, her mouth open but silent, whatever sound there might have been now lost. He grabbed her arms and held them until she had her balance, and still holding her, his fingers constricting her thin arms, he said, "Hell, relax, Sis. I'm fine."

"Eddie, let go. You're hurting me," she said.

He looked down at her, and she couldn't see anything in his eyes that she understood, but again she couldn't make a sound.

"Sorry," he said, letting go of her and slumping back onto the car seat.

"God, I wish you wouldn't act that way, Eddie," she said, breathing hard.

"Okay, Sis. I won't," he said, smiling at her, his thin lips parting to show his large yellow teeth. "I was just kidding, Sis. Hey, it's been great hunting. Nothing like a Hoover Steak, right?"

"When Mr. Roosevelt is elected, we won't have to come out here to do this," Phyllis said, as though she meant to defy someone.

"Ah, hell, Sis, he's just another damn politician. He ain't going to change anything."

"You wait and see, Eddie. When he's elected, everything'll be different. We won't have to poach any deer to live on. You wait and see."

"Hell," he said, turning back to the car. "There's another bottle at the cabin, ain't there?"

Ring surged past him and jumped over the edge of the bank into the draw. The big Irish setter bounded up to Davey, who was pulling the headless carcass of the doe down the slope into the bottom of the draw. The dog started to sniff and paw at the dead animal. "C'mon, Ring. Back off," Davey said, dropping the doe's legs and taking his felt hat off and wiping his forehead with his hand and then vigorously scratching his head. His light brown hair was damp with sweat from dragging the doe. He looked at Phyllis and smiled, making large dimples in his cheeks. "Got her," he said. "Eddie. C'mere and give me a hand."

"Damnit," Eddie said petulantly, but he stood up, and gaining his equilibrium, he went down the bank.

When the Model T started back down over the ruts of the old wagon road, the sun came up over the curve of the mountain and the dust rose into the golden morning and hung yellow and ethereal. Aspen and willow leaves sparkled like silver coins, and at the beaver dam red-winged blackbirds hovered in the ochre sky and dived toward the Model T as it flounced slowly past them.

At the cabin, Davey and Eddie went around to the back to where two other headless deer hung. They had been hung by their hocks from a pine rail set between two large ponderosa pines. Underneath the two deer was a long, wooden table, and on the table were black starbursts where the two deer had bled their last drops.

Ring went with Davey and Eddie, but Davey said, "Ring. Get away," when the setter crouched to jump onto the table. The dog now stood behind Davey and Eddie and watched them and the two deer with wondering eyes.

When Davey and Eddie dragged the last one past the kitchen door, Eddie said, "I want a drink," and he dropped the leg he was holding.

Davey stopped and looked up. "Let's put this one in the back-seat with the others first," he said.

"No. I want a drink, now."

"The bottle's in on the cupboard counter."

When Eddie came out of the kitchen, he had the unlabeled bottle of clear liquid in his hand. He stood like a sentry on the kitchen steps, threw his head back, tilted the bottle, and drove the neck into his lips. His Adam's apple bobbed up and down as he swallowed. He lowered the bottle, and held it at his side, and with his eyes closed he stood as though he meant to be immobile the rest of this life.

When he finally opened his eyes, he breathed hard and murmured something Davey couldn't hear, and then he looked down at Davey and said, "Good." His voice was flat but decisive.

They wrapped the three headless deer in a canvas tarp and shoved them down on the floor behind the front seat. Phyllis had retreated into the cabin, and Davey followed to wash up and change clothes.

When they came out of the cabin, the day hung from the sun, azure and brilliant. Phyllis wore a cotton print dress flowered with violets, and her dark hair glistened, every curl lying smooth and placid around her angular face. She wore cotton stockings and black shoes with heels and straps. Davey had changed from his blood blackened bibs into a clean white shirt, tan cotton pants, and tan leather Oxfords. He had on a red bow tie. When Phyllis saw Eddie sitting on the hood of the Model T with the bottle again in his hand, she drew back close to Davey, hanging against him as if she wanted to grow onto him like a vine to a trellis.

"Let's get this meat back to Cheyenne, Eddie," Davey said.

Eddie didn't speak. He slid off the hood of the Model T and walked back along the side of the car, now hot from sitting in the sun, and sagged like a loose bundle against the door. "Maybe I'm not ready to go, yet," he said, his words sliding against one another.

"Please, Eddie," Phyllis said.

"C'mon, Eddie. We don't want to get caught with this stuff. Once we get to the highway, we'll be okay," Davey said.

"I don't give a damn," Eddie said, slurring the words, his eyes blinking. "I ain't ready."

"C'mon, Eddie," Davey said.

Eddie opened the car door and set the bottle down on the floor and pulled one of the rifles off the front seat. He turned around and said, "I ain't ready, yet. I'm going hunting." He sounded almost surprised at the sound of his own voice, as if something wonderful had just occurred to him.

"Hunting's over, Eddie," Davey said, finally beginning to understand how drunk Eddie was. Davey reached out and put his hand on the rifle.

"Goddamn you," Eddie said, and he let go of the rifle and turned and pulled another from the front seat, saying, "By, God, when I'm ready to go, I'll let you know about it."

A long, low whine came from Phyllis's open mouth, and her hands reached out in front of her as though she meant to grasp something but there was nothing there.

Eddie levered a shell into the chamber of the rifle and brought the barrel up. There was a terrible report, and Eddie stood still looking at Davey. "My, God, Davey, you shot me," he said with no suggestion of surprise at all. Then he dropped the rifle he was holding and yelled, "My, God, Davey, you shot me! You shot me!" and Phyllis screamed and started to stamp her feet in the dust, and

Ring started to bark, loud snaps of sound, and Davey said, "Hell, yes, I shot you, you damn fool. Shut up. You're not hurt. Phyllis, be quiet. He's not hurt any. Damnit, Ring, be quiet." He reached out to put his arm around Phyllis, and Phyllis started to beat her hands against her legs. Ring kept barking at all of them.

"Good, God, will the three of you quiet down?" Davey said. "Phyllis, he's not hurt. Eddie, you're not hurt. Ring, shut up."

Eddie had slumped to the ground and sat in the dirt watching his sister with a bemused interest, feeling along his arm, which had suddenly become very numb. "Look, Sis, he shot me," he said, turning away and examining his arm, where there was a dark red stain spreading down his shirt sleeve. His rage was drained away; he looked exhausted and purified by its passing.

Davey drew Phyllis away from Eddie and walked her around the Model T, crooning to her all the time, "He's not hurt. I didn't hurt him. He just got a scratch. He'll be okay tomorrow. Sit down here." He guided her back against the fender of the car, laying the rifle on the hood and putting both his hands on her shoulders to steady her, as she looked into his calm gray eyes. Her mouth was open but she was speechless, as though someone had been unexpectedly rude to her.

"There now," he said, handing her a white handkerchief from his back pocket. He went to the cabin and came back with a bed sheet and tore a strip from it. "Hold up your arm," he said to Eddie.

"You shot me," Eddie said, still incredulous. Ring sat next to him, his long, red tail swishing in the dust, panting into Eddie's white face.

"You're not hurt," Davey said, wrapping the strip of sheet around Eddie's arm and over the big red stain on his shirt. "Your sister's hurt more than you are. Be quiet and keep your mouth shut. Damnit, Ring, get away."

The inside of the car smelled of whiskey, cigarettes, dog, and the strong, tinny odor of dead animals. Between Esterbrook and Glendo, Davey had to stop twice to let Eddie throw up, and when they crossed Elk Horn Creek, Phyllis had to get out of the car, and she fell down in the mud. She cried for the next half hour, and her mascara ran until she looked like she had painted her face with two large, black stripes that ran from her eyes down her cheeks. When they drove into Glendo, Davey said, "I'm going to get a sundae."

Glendo ripened in the sun on both sides of the dirt highway that ran through the middle of the town. On one side there were small houses and a frame hotel and a grocery store, all of them frame constructions painted white. On the other side there was a stucco motor court, a frame restaurant, the frame post office, a frame drugstore, and a stone gas station, all of them painted white, with the lone exception of the pink motor court that had a line of wilting Russian olives in its dusty, gravelly yard.

In the large front windows of the drugstore were cardboard signs with sparklingly pretty young women drinking Coca-Cola from bottles and smiling at the same time.

"I can't go in this way," Phyllis said.

"Sure you can. Here, let me help you," Davey said, taking the handkerchief from her hand and daubing at her face with it, smiling at her all the time. "There you go. C'mon."

Her eyes were red. "Will Eddie be all right?"

Eddie was asleep, curled up next to Ring, both of them lying on top of deer carcasses smelling muskily obscene.

"Who'd bother with that mess?" Davey said, taking Phyllis's hand. The inside of the drugstore was dark and still, and overhead was a large fan that turned slowly with a steady, methodical clack. The soda fountain was at the end of the room and to get to it a person had to walk between glass cases containing bottles of medicinal fluids, pocketknives, chewing tobacco, a rack of threads all the colors of the known world, and a shelf of barn paint. There were three small tables with white synthetic marble tops, like the soda fountain top, and the chairs at the tables and stools at the soda fountain were wrought iron.

"You folks sure look hot," a woman behind the soda fountain called to them. Mrs. Wright was a small, gray-haired woman with finger curls, who looked like she should be the mother of all of the sparkling young women drinking Coca-Cola. Her movements were small, quick, like a sparrow hopping.

"You bet we are," Davey said, smiling at the woman, letting her see his bluish gray eyes, his grin, unalarming and virginal. "And we'd like a couple of sundaes." Phyllis, despite all her misery, had to squeeze his arm affectionately. Even in her misery she was defenseless against his bubbling, innocent charm.

"Well, you just come right up here, then. Been a time on the road?"

"Just came in from Esterbrook," Davey said. "Been sightseeing. What kind of sundae do you want, Honey?"

"Chocolate. Oh, please, do you have some place I could freshen up?"

"Why, sure thing, Honey. Right back through that curtain. You'll find the place. How about you, Mister?"

"Marshmallow," Davey said.

When they came out of the drugstore, a game warden was looking in the car window, his long body bent at his waist and his knees bent, too. Ring was standing in the backseat looking at the warden, his rudderlike tail sweeping back and forth in lazy strokes as though he were fanning himself, his pink tongue hanging loosely out of his mouth, his eyes questioning. When he saw Davey, he barked with a silly glee. The game warden, without straightening, looked around at Davey and Phyllis.

Davey and Phyllis both stood stiffly. The game warden straightened and said, "Your car stinks."

"My God, I'm glad we found you," Davey said, and he walked briskly, with a heavy assumption of purpose, to the game warden, leaving Phyllis standing on the sidewalk with her mouth open. "Those people shot my girlfriend's brother. See?" he said, leaning down and looking through the window and pointing at the sleeping figure of Eddie under Ring's feet. "Get out of the way, Ring. Stop standing on poor Eddie. Poachers, by golly."

"Poachers?"

"Yes, sir," Davey said, looking up at the game warden. The warden was very young, and the only way Davey had known he was a game warden was because of the unmistakable little badge on his clean white shirt. He had brown eyes that reminded Davey of Ring's eyes, dreamy and imploring. He was very thin, and his face was very smooth. He looked as though he might at any minute blush, and there was no way to know whether he was strong.

"I'll go to the hotel and call the sheriff's office in Wheatland, Mister."

"I have to get him to a doctor, Warden. You better call the sheriff in Douglas, too, and maybe the sheriff in Laramie. Hard saying where those murderers went to."

"Is he dead?"

"No. Just wounded. Just his arm, he'll be fine. But they were trying to kill us. We captured the evidence, though." Davey opened the car door and Ring jumped out and sat on the street, looking from Davey to the warden with an expectant interest. The odor was malignant and powerful, but Davey reached in and called, "Eddie! Eddie! Wake up. We've got to give this evidence to the warden, Eddie."

"My name's Elliott Clagett," the warden said.

Davey turned around and shook Clagett's outstretched hand. "Glad to meet you, Clagett."

Eddie sat up. He smelled evil. Davey reached in and pulled him by his good arm toward the open door, and his body flopped loosely over the deer. Eddie tried to understand what was happening and he faintly called out, "I want my sister." Davey continued to drag him out of the open door. Eddie flowed down into the street next to Ring. Without pausing, Davey threw back the canvas and wrenched at one of the deer's legs, jerking it spasmodically out the open door to where it also collapsed into the street.

"What are you doing?" Clagett asked.

"Help me with this deer," Davey said, pulling at another one of the does.

"What about him?" Clagett asked, pointing down at Eddie, who was stretched out full length on his back in the street, a soapy film bubbling around his partially open mouth.

"Don't worry about him. He's asleep," Davey said. "C'mon. Grab this leg."

They pulled the doe out of the car and laid the carcass next to the first one. Then they pulled the third one out of the car and let it flop down with the other two.

"You can have the tarp, too," Davey said, taking it out of the car and spreading it over the carcasses, already trapping black flies under it.

"He doesn't look very well to me," Clagett said.

"Drunk. Had to get him drunk to kill the pain." They both looked down at Eddie. "Pitiful, isn't it?" Davey said.

"Real shame. I'll call the sheriff. He'll probably want to talk to you."

"I have to get him to a doctor. Probably go to Casper. Tell him he can catch us there."

"You're the fellow who bought that cabin up on Rooper's place, aren't you?"

Davey turned around and looked at Phyllis. He took his hat off and wiped his forehead, and finally said, "Yeah." Then he said, "C'mon, Honey. We've got to get Eddie to the doctor." He held out his hand, helped Phyllis into the street, and opened the car door for her.

She paused and looked down at Eddie. "God, he looks dead."

"He's all right," Davey said. "Mr. Clagett'll help me put him in the backseat. Don't worry about him."

"Oh, poor Eddie. He really does look dead," she said.

"He's just fine. He's just passed out, that's all," Davey said. "Poachers," he said, looking at Clagett.

"Poachers," Clagett said, and both of them nodded as though together they had discovered something of consequence that no one else knew about.

Just before they started up the big hill at the south edge of town, Davey asked, "Is the warden still back there?"

Phyllis turned around and looked. "Yes."

"What's he doing?"

"He's just standing there in the street watching us."

"Wave at him."

Phyllis leaned out the window, and looking back as the wind blew her hair back over her head, she waved vigorously.

"What's he doing?" Davey asked.

"Waving." When she stopped waving and turned around, she said, "I don't like this. We were lucky as hell to get out of it."

"Lucky, did you say, 'Lucky?' Kiddo, we aren't lucky. He knows we're guilty as sin; he just can't prove anything on us. He'll be watching us for the rest of his life. You can bet on it, Kiddo."

"Well, I didn't have any fun, and I don't want to do this again. My, God, poor Eddie."

"We'll go to a show when we get to Cheyenne. You'll like that, won't you?"

"That'll be fun. Then let's have a party, Davey."

"You got it, Kiddo."

And Then . . .

The Contest

Lucille

Well, I knew something was wrong when I looked up and saw Leaky coming across the street in the middle of the day, and, of course, I'm a good news type of person, so the first thing that went through my mind was, "Maybe his damn wife has died, finally. Maybe she finally wound up getting pregnant just too many times, and she finally just up and died."

The Good Lord knows I waited long enough for that to happen. Well, that's what love does to you. If you fall in love—and the Good Lord knows I fell in love with that silly Leaky—you wait for the man's wife to die, hoping every day of your life that she will fall down some steps or get run over or something. I know it might not be nice to think that way, but every time I went to church I prayed for her to get herself killed somehow, anyway, I didn't care what way.

I prayed and waited for ten years for her to get herself killed. Good Lord, I even would have been happy for just a good disease to have come along and killed her. Oh, Leaky would have been heartbroken, because in his way he loved her too, and I sure would have felt sorry for that little bastard, too, but the Good Lord knows I sure would have comforted that little baby. And I would really have felt sorry for all them kids losing their mother, because I know it's hard for a child to lose their mother, the Good Lord knows I know that. Good Lord, I've thought sometimes I would go crazy growing up with my daddy and taking care of him all these years, sweet darling that he is, but I would have made losing their mother up to them.

I don't know why some people think it's so damn easy to be in love with another woman's husband. Some people think all you have to do is hold open the door for them, lie down and take it from them, get up and hold the door open for them again. Well, there's just a hell of a lot more to it than that. Think of everything I had to give up. When my best friends were getting married and divorced and playing around, what did I get? Nothing. I got a big nothing. I finally got so I wouldn't even go to a friend's wedding because it just got to be too embarrassing to catch that silly-assed bouquet all the time, and then stand there and blush with all those people staring at me, and the Good Lord knows that I knew just what they were thinking, too, especially the men. That's another thing, too. The men. They all think that because I crawl into bed with one woman's husband, that I'll crawl into bed with any damn woman's husband who happens to come into the lounge, slobbering all over the bar, or who comes knocking at my door at two o'clock in the morning, drunk on his stupid ass. And children. Well, I never had any children. I love children. I always wanted to have children. Well, when you're in love with another woman's husband, you can't have any children. Oh, I know, some women do, but they are just plain dirty. I wouldn't ever have done anything like that to poor Leaky. The Good Lord knows poor Leaky had enough problems of his own without my going and delivering up to him another baby to support. He and that woman he was married to had enough children, as it was. To look at her, I guess she couldn't do anything more than have babies. But for Leaky, I went barren. I was in love with that poor little bastard, and don't I know it.

Leaky came across the street in little spurts. He stood against that jaundiced Model A he drove and waited for a car to drive past him, and then he came forward a little and had to wait until another car went by, and then he came a little more across the street, like he wasn't sure he either should be doing it or could do it, but that was Leaky. He wasn't exactly a fireball of a personality.

I've often wondered why I was so in love with him, and damned if I don't think it was the way he looked sad all the time, like his mother had just died or something. I sure as hell didn't love him for his money. Here it was 1947 and Leaky was driving a brokenspirited car that was twenty years old. It might have been one of the first ones ever made, but the Good Lord knows he didn't have it when it was new. He barely had it when it was old. He barely had anything but kids and the equipment to make them with. Well, he could have done better if that woman he was married to wouldn't have kept having all those babies. It seems that she would have taken more of an interest in him and his situation, if she had loved him. I guess I was just a sucker for the way he looked all the time, and I just couldn't help myself when I looked at him, and all I ever wanted to do was just baby the poor little bastard. He had the biggest brown eyes, and he always looked like he was wondering at the world itself, as if the whole thing of life was a mystery, and he didn't have the slightest idea of what was happening, like he just put his foot off the edge of the world and didn't know what to do next. For all he worked out there in the timber, his face was just as smooth as my leg, and I use lotion on my legs every night, I want you to know. I believe a woman should take the best care of herself for her man. You'd think that a man who worked in the timber would have to have big, gnarly hands, but Leaky's hands were small, as though they had been carved from ivory, and they were so white, not like you would think they would be. He didn't really seem to tan at all. His whole body was just kind of smooth and white, even his feet that were too big for the rest of him. They say if you have big feet, then you're going to be big.

Well, they missed on Leaky. He had the big feet, but that was about all that was big, except you know what.

He was dressed like he always was. His old, brown, lace-up work shoes with those thick, black rubber soles that looked like snowshoes on him, and he walked like he was stepping over things all the time, or trying not to step in something, if you know what I mean. He had on a worn-out pair of faded, blue denim coveralls and a blue denim shirt, and his brown hair hung over his pretty, white forehead, just kind of tumbling out from under his hat, that old, gray hat with the brim turned down in front that looked like a cow had decided it hadn't liked it and had stomped it good. He looked just like a bum in the movies. I guess Leaky could have put on a new suit and still looked like he just crawled off the flatcar, the Good Lord love him.

Before he got to the front door of the lounge, he disappeared from the window where I had been standing watching him come across the street, so I turned and watched the door, and here he came. He came in like a deer does when he comes to water. Kind of looking around, stepping hesitantly, sniffing the air, so to speak, like he wasn't sure just what might be there in the dark.

I just stood behind the bar and waited. There wasn't anything else I could do. I had paying customers there at the bar who expected me to serve them when they were ready to be served. Leaky came up to the bar and sat down as though he were going to pose for a picture. He smelled tinny and hard, like he had been soldered together with pitch. I knew he didn't have a cent on him. He looked right at me with those eyes like big peonies. If he had money he didn't look right at anyone. He always looked like he couldn't have cared less. But when he was broke, he always looked right at me, as if he were facing up to something and wanted to make a straight go of it, as though he just had come from a church and had looked on the pearls of Heaven. I just turned around and went to my tip jar that I always kept just under the row of imported whiskeys (I don't touch anything in it for a week at a time, and then I'm always happy when I find how much I have made in tips. It just makes me feel better doing it that way. Kind of like a Christmas present once a week.) and took out several ones—I didn't count them because I didn't want to, but I'd have done anything for the poor little bastard—and walked down to the end of the bar, and Leaky got down off the stool and came down to the end of the bar. I said as low as I could so I wouldn't attract any more attention than Leaky and I had already, "What in the name of the Good Lord are you doing here?"

"I need a loan," he whispered. The sound of his voice was like a razor being stropped.

"I figured it was money. How much and what for?" I asked. After all, it was going to be my money, and he was my boyfriend. I had every right to know.

"I need yer daddy's shotgun, too," he said.

"What?" I asked. I couldn't believe I heard him.

"I need five dollars and yer daddy's shotgun," he said.

He was looking right at me. His big, pretty brown eyes looked as sad as I had ever seen them, like he was laboring under a permanent grievance, and I think he could do that to me on purpose whenever he wanted to. I said, "Baby, what in the hell do you want with Daddy's shotgun?"

"I'm goin' huntin'," he said. His eyes were as innocent as pet dog's.

"Baby, you haven't ever been hunting in your life. Why are you going hunting? Are you sure you're going hunting?" I was beginning to worry, now. Leaky? Hunting? My Good Lord, he's going to kill someone, I thought. Then I started wondering who he was going to kill. Leaky was so harmless, no one ever really got mad at him about anything because they knew it wouldn't have done any good. I just couldn't picture Leaky pointing a shotgun at anyone. That someone just wouldn't come into focus. Even his damned wife wouldn't show up in my mind, that's how harmless I knew Leaky was.

"Shore, I'm goin' huntin'," he said. "Yer daddy got any shells for that shotgun? I'll need some shells for it," he said.

"Baby, why are you going hunting? There isn't any hunting season going on." Now, my Daddy was a hunter, and I had grown up knowing about hunting, and this was the middle of summer, and there wasn't any hunting season anywhere in the middle of the summer, and so that meant Leaky was going to go poaching instead, and I wasn't about to have any boyfriend of mine do anything like that.

He looked right at me. "Don't say nothin'?"

"You tell me, Leaky, and you tell me now," I said, "and you hurry up, because I got customers."

"Don't be so loud," he said. "Ol' man Sturgis is goin' to hold a quail hunt on his land and there's goin' to be a prize for the guy who gits the most quail," he whispered.

"There aren't any quail in the state, Leaky," I said.

"Ol' man Sturgis brung 'em in. He's goin' to let 'em loose out at his ranch. You got to pay to enter," he said.

"Wait a minute," I said. "First, you got to pay to enter an illegal hunt; second, if you win the illegal hunt, you win all the illegal money that was paid in illegal entries; and, third, you got all the illegal quail, too. Is that right?"

"Kinda," he said. He said it the way someone might talk about the weather.

"It's a hell of a lot more than 'kinda,' Leaky. You're gonna get your sweet little ass thrown in jail for even showing up at Sturgis's place. Where the hell did you hear about this, anyway?"

Leaky just stared at me. "You know Dandy's cuttin' timber on Sturgis's place. Well, Dandy was there when Sturgis set this up, and Dandy was talkin' about it this mornin'. I gotta git out there, Honey. I can win more money shootin' a few little ol' quail than I can make in six months skiddin' logs for Dandy. C'mon, Honey."

That poor little bastard was the saddest looking son-of-a-bitch I ever saw in my life. My Good Lord, but I loved Leaky. When I think of him standing there, not really asking for anything I couldn't do for him, I still just about swoon. He was the prettiest person I ever saw in my life.

"All right," I said. I was almost panting, I was so hot.

"Yer a sweetie," he said. His smile made his mouth look like a shattered window.

Good Lord, I loved that man.

Mazell

My God, how the hell was I supposed to know that dumb bastard was going to be standin' right there? My God, he could have been standin' in a hundred other places just as well, and he chose to stand right there.

He drove up in that dilapidated, old Model A with his whole family packed into it, kids' heads and arms and legs stickin' out of it all over like it was some kind of a ruined pin cushion that someone probably threw away. His missus was sittin' in the front seat, one little girl squnched down between her and that dumb bastard pa of hers and her mother holdin' that baby, the only boy in the family, on her lap, two other girls in the backseat, and two more in that wood box rumble seat he built to hold all of them, every one of them a towhead.

She was a pretty woman, kind of. She looked like old wash hung out to dry, but she had that soft, blond hair that she wore kind of long and fluffy and glisteny, and her skin was smooth, and that was the damnedest thing. Most women that had been through all the kids she had been through and lived the way she did in that clapboard and tarpaper shack like all the rest of those sawmillers, washin' clothes and kids, and cleanin'—because she did keep a clean place, even if it was nothin' but a damn shack—cookin' and probably sawmillin' too, although I never heard of her doin' it, but knowin' that damn Leaky, I wouldn't a been surprised to know she did most of that, too, and all of it done in blowin' sand, too, would have looked like a worn out gunnysack.

She was wearin' a white and blue flower print dress that was just about as down and out as that old Model A he drove, made of feed sacks that she had begged for at every feed store in town to clothe her and all those little girls. She had a decent figure, yet, even after all those kids of hers and Leaky, but she wasn't a Hollywood starlet. She was thin, like maybe she was bein' drained of her juices, and her eyes were so light and clear you wondered how much left she had to be drained of. Oh, maybe her nose was a little big, but the more you were around her the less you thought of it that way. Yes, she was kind of a pretty woman. A delicate woman, you might say, like an old china teacup.

All those little girls, fortunately, looked like her more than they looked like Leaky. They all had that soft blond hair just like her and big brown eyes like Leaky, so they carried that much of him around with them, but it didn't seem to hurt them any. All of 'em were pretty damn skinny, and you always wondered how much they got to eat.

You couldn't tell anything about that little baby boy, but you sure worried about him growin' up to be another damn Leaky.

Well, anyway, there they were.

Leaky got out of the Model A and walked over to Buck and said, "I got an entry fee." He sounded like a preacher who had just summed up all Hell for everyone and wasn't goin' to let any of 'em forget it, either.

Buck looked down at Leaky. His eyes were like lead pennies. Then he said, "Hell, Leaky, you aren't any hunter. You haven't ever hunted anything. Quail are hard to hunt. They're harder to shoot. You sure you got five dollars?" he said loud, the way he said everything, like he was always having to yell at a slow cow. He threw his hands around when he talked like he was trying to dry them.

"I got the entry fee," Leaky said. His brown eyes were floating over Buck's face, missing his eyes every time, and he kind of jutted forward, like he was watchin' something real close.

Buck kind of turned around and looked at the rest of us standin' there, like he wanted someone to get him outta this mess, like a man troubled by a suggested threat, but we didn't say anything. None of us cared whether or not Leaky wanted to hunt for the prize, because we knew he wasn't a hunter, and we knew he didn't know beans about what he was supposed to do. He wasn't goin' to take any prize money from anyone, unless there was a contest for bein' a fool, and then no one in their right mind would've even tried against him.

"Let's see it, Leaky," Buck said.

Leaky dug a five-dollar bill out his coverall pocket and put it right up to Buck, and Buck took it and looked at it and looked at Leaky. Buck looked like he had been handed a summons to court.

That was when Leaky's wife came up to him and with her shoulder—she was holdin' that baby boy all wrapped in a shabby baby blanket that I'm sure someone had given to her a long time ago—and kind of motioned him away. He stepped away from all of us and leaned up to her, and we all heard her say, "Lord, Leaky, don't do this. If you really got five dollars, we need it. Give me the five dollars, Leaky, and let's go home." Her voice sounded like a sheet being dragged over a bed.

"No. I come out here to hunt and win a prize. I ain't goin' home," he said.

"Leaky, you haven't got any business doin' this," she said.

"I know just what I'm doin'," he said, which set a record, because this was the first time he ever knew what he was doin'.

"Please," she said. She looked frayed and exhausted, as though speaking would have to be accomplished through invention and patience. Her voice was like a plaintive call for a lost child.

"No. You git back in that car and wait," he said, and he turned around and walked back to us, where we were all standin' lookin' at the sky or ground or anything but them. It was embarrassin' as hell to have to listen to all that. He shouldn't have brought her. No one else brought their wives, for Christ's sake.

She didn't give up. She walked right up to Buck, who looked like he wanted to go huntin' hisself, and right then, too. He didn't even bother to look at her when she came right up to him and looked at him. "Don't take his money, Mister Sturgis," she said. "He don't know what he's doin'," she said.

"None of my business," Buck said, still not lookin' at her.

"You know he don't know what he's doin'," she said.

"If he's got the money, he can enter, just like anybody else," Buck said. Buck wasn't goin' to let anybody tell him anything, and he just got stubborn, and I had to look away before I laughed at him for gettin' hisself into the jam he was in. Buck had all the flexibility of iron, and I knew he wasn't goin' to back down then or any other time, whether or not he thought Leaky had any business bein' out there huntin' his quail in a contest or otherwise. All that poor woman did was make it certain that Leaky was goin' to hunt them quail.

Well, she went back over to that old Model A and sat down in the front seat and stayed there like she was a part of the vehicle itself, stiff and angular and tired like a bucket that had carried anything and everything. Those little girls stayed right there, too, except where she didn't look neither right nor left, but just straight ahead, they was cranin' all over to see everything that was goin' on, and where their daddy was goin'.

Well, I didn't think anymore about that damn fool Leaky. I figured he was old enough to do whatever he wanted and whatever he wanted was his business and not mine.

I hadn't ever hunted any quail. None of us had. We all hunted grouse for birds or maybe some ducks, but in that country, there weren't very damn many ducks to hunt, because there wasn't any damn water for them to set on. When a duck come through, we all went to the well and put out a bucket of water for him and called all the kids around to come see him.

Hunting those grouse was a pretty easy deal. Sage grouse just sat still and stared straight ahead, except for the younger ones, and they would finally panic and run, and then you knew where they all were, and so you could just wait for them to raise out of the sagebrush and take 'em, one at a time like tin cans on a fence, except that they would be flyin', like B-17s, comin' low over the sagebrush like they was on a low level bombin' run or somethin'.

The blue grouse, they would be so kind as to just fly up in a tree and sit there, and if a guy had a twenty-two pistol, he could just stand there and get what he wanted, because they didn't have anymore sense than to just keep sittin' there on a tree limb starin' off into the distance like they was watchin' something long past and tryin' to understand it, until there weren't any of 'em left.

That's how you shoot chickens and grouse. But the trick was to find the damn things first. Sometimes those sage grouse wouldn't budge, no matter what, and if they didn't, you could walk right past them and not ever know it. Those silly, damn blue grouse might pick a tree a million yards way, too, and then you'd be runnin' after 'em all day and might never catch up to 'em. Nope. You had to be real careful huntin' any of 'em.

Well, these here quail we had heard was somethin' different. That's why Buck had gone and got them. Well, that wasn't the only reason. You'd better believe that if Buck went and bought a bunch of quail, he was goin' to make money off 'em. Buck wasn't the type of person who just did somethin' because he thought it was goin' to be a lot of fun to do or a good thing to do. Buck hadn't got his ranch built up to where it was by being a damn fool about money. We all of us, except, I suppose, that dumb bastard Leaky, knew that we might get to have a good time and maybe one of us would win some money, but we all of us knew that Buck was gettin' something if not plenty out of the whole shebang.

Buck didn't inherit his ranch. He was nothin' but a cowboy without a daddy. He worked like hell from the time he was just a kid and saved his money. When we'd all go to the Saturday night dance, Buck would stay at the ranch and wash his clothes, and pack wood and string more fence for more money. He just sat and collected money, and when he was twenty, he went to a Saturday night dance, all right, but he went to dance with Mary Albright, and he danced just one evening with her and married her the next weekend, and a week later he bought his parcel of land with her old man's money.

He never bought anything else that wasn't land or had four legs. Nossir. If Buck was throwin' a party for everyone, he was gettin' something out of it, you better believe it, but we all knew that, so we didn't care. We all just came for the fun of it, and watchin' Buck tangle with Leaky's wife and gettin' hisself hooked into lettin' Leaky hunt was worth the whole thing to all of us.

Well, the first damn quail I saw was just a wish. Up to then the fastest thing I'd ever seen was a Goddamn Messerschmitt comin' over a line of trees and aimin' right at me, but let me tell you, that quail made nothin' but a damn fool out of any Goddamn Kraut Messerschmitt I ever saw. That quail flew from one side of the creek to the other and was gone so damn fast I never even raised my twenty gauge. Zip. He was gone.

So I just kept goin' down the creek. I was walkin' just under the high water mark and where I could see a good piece in front of me without them willows and cottonwoods gettin' in my way, steppin' real easy and watchin' close.

Here come another one, only he was flyin' right straight at me, right above the creek, and when he got next to me I was ready and I fired and missed by a mile, and that's when I heard someone sound like they were stranglin'.

Well, I ran through them willows and across the creek, and here was that damn fool Leaky, thrashin' in the grass. He was covered with blood. Hell, there was blood everywhere—on the grass, on his shirt and coveralls, on his face—hell, you couldn't see his face for all the blood.

"Well, shit!" I said.

Hell, I didn't know that dumb bastard was anywhere around.

Buck

I just had this feeling, that was all. As soon as I let that sorry God-damn Leaky shoulder that shotgun he had borrowed from Lucille's father—my God, he borrowed the shotgun from his mistress's father and brought his family along to watch—and as soon as he started down the creek, I just had this feeling that something was going to happen to ruin that day. Don't ask me how I knew that, I just did. It was like something dark crawled over my navel.

When I think about everything that happened to me that day, I wish I had that sorry little son-of-a-bitch right here in my hands.

I had to go clear to Nebraska to get those quail. I drove all the way to Columbus without stopping for anything but gas and a sandwich in Ogallala, that cost me almost twenty-five cents, and that was when I just about made up my mind that those people in Nebraska weren't anything but a bunch of damn crooks. It was a hamburger with mustard and pickle, and little pile of potato chips none of 'em not any bigger than a bull rider's rowel. Shouldn't have cost more than fifteen cents. That was before I got to Columbus and that fellow's farm where he had those quail. Oh, they were all boxed up and ready to go, all right, but when I got there was when I found out that there was a trucking fee from Iowa that I was going to get stuck with, too, and that's when I knew all those people in Nebraska weren't anything but a bunch of damn crooks, and they knew they had me, too, and a person oughtn't to run it over a fellow that way.

Those quail, and there were only a hundred of them, cost me a dollar apiece.

That was on top of the gas and the sandwich, and you have to know that trip didn't do my International any good, either, and that includes the tires, too.

I knew about quail. Those little birdies are so damn fast these grouse hunters were going to spin like tops and do just as much damage, too. I knew that these grouse hunters who think they're so damn good were going to have one hell of a time hitting any of those little devils, so I passed the word out all around to everyone I could think of who wouldn't go blab it all to every damn game warden in the country that I was going to have a prize hunt. When it was all over I had fifty hunters there for that prize hunt. I gave the winner fifty dollars, too. A man has to find a way to get along in this world.

I mean I not only had to go to Nebraska to get taken in by those damn crooks, but I was putting myself on the line, because bringing those quail into the state was illegal as hell, even if I was going to put them on my land and hunt them on my land, which shouldn't have been anyone's business but mine. But, oh, no. If any of those damn game wardens ever got wind of what we were going to do out on the ranch, you can just bet they would have wailed loud enough to have roused whales in the ocean, and those Nebraska crooks knew it, too.

But having a prize hunt seemed like a good idea to me, and it would have been a good idea except for that sorry damn fool Leaky showing up, and my letting him go out there. But I figure if a man has an entry fee, he can get in the race. What happens to him in the race is his problem.

I sent the hunters out in pairs, one on one side of the creek, the other on the other side. Two hunters should know how to hunt like that, and there were all these hotshot grouse hunters there with their hotshot shotguns that I figured they ought to be able to take care of themselves. That's why I paired up Mazell with that sorry son-of-a-bitch Leaky. Mazell was a war hero. He killed a bunch of those Kraut sons-of-bitches with that rifle of his, and I figured that if anyone could take care of himself and Leaky at the same time, it would be Mazell.

That was something no one could have counted on. If I had done that a hundred times, nothing would have happened, but this one time, this one, was the wrong one. It seems that everything I did that day just added up to what happened. It was like it didn't make any difference what I did, it just turned against me.

Mazell came running back up the creek, and that was when I knew something was going wrong.

"Shit, oh, shit, Buck, I shot him," Mazell said to me. His voice had a soprano quality to it, and when he talked he puffed like a child blowing dandelion seeds. His face looked like a man who had just been unreasonably whipped, and his eyes looked like porcelain dishes.

"Shot who?" I asked, but I knew who he had shot, and I was already looking over at that junk Model A with her sitting there staring straight ahead and those kids playing in the dirt right next to the Model A. My stomach already was beginning to whine a little, like maybe something wasn't quite right down there, like I had eaten rotten peaches.

"Leaky. I shot Leaky," he said to me.

"Is he dead?" I asked. Just what I needed—a dead hunter on an illegal hunt. The Goddamn game wardens would love this one.

"No. But he's pretty bad off. We'd better get down there and get him back up here, Buck. He's hurt real bad. I've seen stuff like this before, and I know he's hurt pretty damn bad," he said to me. His whole body seemed to be quivering with some kind of an expectation, the way the sky does when there's lightning. He smelled rank like wet hay.

Mazell was sweating. I couldn't figure out whether it was from running back up the creek or because he was nervous about Leaky. I didn't need a nervous hunter around the place right then, but there wasn't but me and him and Jim Starbuck and Henry Stanton standing there. We all walked down the creek to where Leaky was lying in the grass. He didn't have much of a face left that I could see and there was blood all over the grass and soaking into the dust and he was covered with the stuff. I could feel my stomach stewing.

"Holy shit!" Henry said. "Hell, he's a goner. Is he still breathing?" His voice was like sand pouring. Nothing on Henry moved. He just stood there like he was going to wait for winter and then might not move, either.

"Well, Mazell, is he still breathing?" I asked. I wasn't about to touch the sorry little son-of-a-bitch.

Mazell got down and felt through the blood for his heart, and then he looked up and said, "Shit, Buck. The bastard died on me." He sounded just like a man whose dog has bit him for no reason.

We walked back up to the ranch house, and I called Doc Mason in town and told him to come out to the ranch because we had an accident, and then I went down to the corral and saddled one horse and took another one, and we all went back down to the creek where that sorry little bastard was, and all the time she just sat there in that damn Model A and didn't say anything, and I don't know if she suspected anything or not. You couldn't tell what she was thinking the way she just sat there like a stone monument to womanhood with little kids climbing all over her like ants over a piece of dry and crustless bread.

I couldn't believe that anyone so little could be so heavy. It took all four of us to lift him onto that horse and tie him down so he wouldn't slide off, because that damn horse sure as hell didn't want that sorry son-of-a-bitch on him, and once we had him half tied on and that horse took to bucking and plunging and snorting and throwed him clear off even with me holding the hackamore rope, and we had to start all over with him dripping blood on every one of us and that spooked up, jugheaded horse, too. I didn't know anything so little as he was could have that much blood in it, and I've drained many a deer in my time. Mazell said, "Yeah. When they're dead, they're real hard to lift. They're always that way." I guess he should know, because he's certainly lifted more dead men than any of us had.

So we finally got him tied down and the horse quieted, even though all the time we towed that horse up to the back door of the ranch—we couldn't just take that sorry son-of-a-bitch in through the front door with her just sitting there in that damn Model A right at the front porch to the house. He kept looking back and snorting and prancing like he was in a parade or something and was the star attraction.

By the time we got him laid out on the kitchen floor with an old tarp under him—I wasn't about to let the sorry little bastard to bleed all over my floor. My God, you can't get blood off a floor, no matter how hard you scrub—Doc Heller drove up in that new Buick of his and parked right next to that disgraceful Model A, and if those two weren't a pair. I almost laughed out loud. Doc looked about as good as that new Buick of his, like he had just been polished.

Doc Heller came into the kitchen and took one look at Leaky and asked, "What'd you call me for? I'm not a miracle man," he said, having brought with him all the way from town that refined haughtiness of his that I didn't really need just then, but I didn't say anything to him about it. He had brazen, diamond clear eyes, and his words sounded like they had been mixed with gravel.

"I didn't know who else to call," I said.

"Try the county coroner," he said. "What happened?"

"He got shot," Mazell said. He leaned against the jamb and he looked like his bones were melting.

"Good, God, Mazell, I can see that. How'd he get shot?"

"Accident," Mazell said.

Doc looked up at Mazell and held him right there, and then he glanced at me, but by God I kept looking at Mazell. It was bad enough having the sorry little bastard killed on my place without me taking the blame for it. "Mazell?" he asked.

"We were just doing some shooting, and I didn't know the damned fool had walked down right in front of where I was shooting," Mazell said.

Doc didn't say anything about that. Then he said, "Well, I'll call Butch and tell him he's got a carcass out here. What'd his wife say?"

"She doesn't know yet," I said.

"Good Christ, Buck. She doesn't know about this?"

"Nope," I said.

"Good Christ," he said again, and he turned and left, and I heard the door close, so I figured he went out to tell her. A minute later I heard him come back in and call Butch to bring the wagon out and get the little bastard off my kitchen floor. I got a bottle of Old Overholt out of the cupboard and some glasses and poured everyone a drink, and we stood around and stared at that Goddamn Leaky, no one saying anything, I suppose everyone thinking about him in their own way, me thinking I would strangle him if I could. After a while I heard a knock on my front screen, and I looked out there, and there she was standing there. I went to the screen and said, "What do you want, Mizzus Johnson?"

"I want to talk to you, Mister Sturgis," she said.

"Talk, then," I said. "We're all real sorry about Leaky, Ma'am."

"I'd like to talk to you out here, Mister Sturgis," she said. She looked as though she were almost too gossamer to speak.

I opened the screen, and she stepped back, tentatively like there might some condition to be observed, and I stepped out on the porch, and said, "All right."

"Mister Sturgis, there's been a terrible thing happen here today," she said.

"Yup," I said.

"Terrible for me and my poor family," she said.

"Yup," I said. What the hell else was I supposed to say? Tell her it was a good thing that it happened because she didn't have to put up with that dumb bastard Leaky anymore?

"Mister Sturgis, I realize that poor Leaky didn't have sense enough to know what he was gettin' himself into, but I want him to have a nice funeral. A nice funeral will be the only thing he ever will have on this earth that will amount to anything."

She just stood there looking at me like I was laundry. "If you don't have any money, the state'll pay something to have him buried," I said.

"Mister Sturgis, perhaps you didn't understand me. If I'm not mistaken, Mister Sturgis, you illegally brought wildlife into the state; you have held an illegal hunt on your land, and a man has been killed, even if that man didn't have any sense at all. I want Leaky to have a nice funeral, Mister Sturgis. I would feel awful good knowin'

Leaky had a nice funeral." Her voice sounded just like her words had been dipped in a honey pot.

That dirty, damn bitch! She stood right there on my front porch and held me up. My God, I thought, why couldn't Mazell have got rid of both them if he was goin' to have an accident?

"Do you understand, Mister Sturgis?" she asked just as pretty-please as she could.

Well, hell, yes, I understood. I understood she probably was descended from some Goddamn Nebraskan; that's what I understood. "Fine," I said. "Is that all?"

"No, sir. I want Leaky's son to go to school. I think you should put a little money aside for him, don't you?"

"What the hell! Listen, lady, I'll be damned if I'm going to stand here and let you rob me just because your damn fool husband didn't have any better sense than to stand in front of a loaded shotgun, you hear?"

I'll be damned if she said anything. She just stood there staring at me like I was a bouquet of flowers.

"I'll put a thousand in for you," I said. "Anything else?"

"Someone'll have to drive us home. I don't know how to drive that awful thing."

"My God."

I swear I could have strangled that sorry little son-of-a-bitch, Leaky!

Leakey's Wife

The funeral was very nice. Poor Leaky would of been very happy if he could of seen it. I don't reckon he ever saw anything like it in his whole life, least as long as I knowed him, he never saw anything like it. I guess the biggest thing he ever saw was a fair with all them rides like the Ferris wheel and them things. We went to one after we was first married. He was so happy takin' me to that fair. We rode all them rides, and we just laughed and laughed. Oh, I was pretty scared when we went up on that Ferris wheel. I hadn't never seen nothing like that before, just a picture or two in some old magazines. It was so wondrous. It looked to be as tall as a bluff along the river. I wanted to scream when we was on top, but I didn't, because Leaky was havin' so much fun and laughin', and I didn't want to cause him no grief. Why, from up there you could see all the lights of Douglas and then some way out, I suppose all the way to Glendo. Probably not Wheatland, though.

We made Lou Lou that night. I knew it, but poor Leaky didn't.

By the time we made Lou Lou and Jenny, we couldn't afford to go to the fair anymore. That almost broke poor Leaky's heart, not bein' able to go to the fair.

We went to dances after we were first married, too. Those were a lot of fun. We used to dance around and around and laugh and laugh like storybook people. We used to walk outside and traipse around behind the dance hall and look at all the stars in the sky. They all looked like little candles up there, and we would try to blow them out, and then we would laugh and laugh, and when we knew no one was lookin', we would squeeze each other a little bit.

We went to the parade when the war was over. Leaky liked that real well. He talked about that for almost a week after it was over. He loved the band music and the soldiers and the flags and all the people that lined the street. He used to sit and tell the kids over and over everything he saw at the parade. It all was like a fair to him.

Poor Leaky thought he was doin' the best thing ever when he went to work, but it turned out to be quite a shock to him. He just never quite got over the jolt that work gave him. After a week, he came home and said he didn't think work was cut out for him and that he probably wasn't goin' to go back, but I talked to him and explained to him that we needed that money he was makin' to live on, 'cause we had Lou Lou on the way. After that he seemed to be all right, though.

Poor Leaky was a good provider, as far as it went. He didn't spend his money on drinkin' the way some men do. I was lucky about that with him; he just didn't care for the taste of the stuff. He didn't spend any money on bettin', either, nor much of anything. If any money was goin' to be spent, I had to do it. I had to buy all the clothes for the little ones, all the groceries for all of us, and even when he got that contraption to drive, I had to go and spend the money for it. Money just didn't seem to make any real sense to poor Leaky.

He was real good to the babies. He used to just play and play with them, and when he had to go to work, sometimes I thought poor Leaky was goin' to cry to have to give up playin' with those little babies. I think a lot of that had to do with poor Leaky not ever quite growin' up hisself. He used to carry on so, runnin' and jumpin' and rollin' right there in the dirt just like the rest of them. He would think of bringin' things, too. He'd bring home old bird nests and rusty things he'd of found along the road and pretty rocks—God, we had rocks in our yard, white ones and red ones and purple ones, and some that were just as clear as any window you'd of ever looked through. If he'd of ever learned to read, he'd of read books to them babies, too, I just know it. Of course, we couldn't of ever afforded any books, but I know he'd of done it.

There were a lot of flowers at the funeral. A lot of gladiolus. White ones and lavender ones and pink ones, and they all smelled like a bottle of perfume left open on a lady's dresser or somethin' to a fresh breeze. Why, when I smelled those flowers, I thought about lacy curtains blowin' away from an open window. The people were all dressed up, and I felt real good about that new, black suit that Leaky was dressed in for the funeral. It was lovely. It was shiny and it had those wide lapels that were so smooth. He had on the blackest tie ever made. The pants didn't let his feet show, thank goodness, 'cause Mister Sturgis said that the suit had cost him enough money, and he wasn't about to buy Leaky any shoes or socks. Leaky hadn't ever had a suit of clothes, not real ones, before, and he would have been shy about goin' to the funeral if he didn't have that new suit of clothes on hisself. The men wore their best boots to the funeral, but I don't suppose Leaky worried too much about his not havin' any new shoes or socks, as he was covered up down there and no one could see whether he did or not. The women were dressed up in black dresses and wore fine, black hats with black veils and black shoes. I wore my new black dress and hat, too, the one Mister Sturgis was so kind to buy for me.

Mister Sturgis was very solemn through the whole funeral. Well, I suppose he should have been since he paid for it.

I wouldn't of minded so much Lucille comin' to the funeral, if she hadn't of sat in the back and cried so loud all the time. It seemed that she could of just left all the cryin' to me and the girls, but she didn't. She started out just snuffin', and that was all right, but after we all sang "That Old Rugged Cross," she started whinin', and then pretty soon she just started crying, and it embarrassed everyone, especially me. Once I thought daddy was goin' to get up and go back there and swear at her, but, thank the Lord, he didn't. Finally, the Reverend Faulkner nodded to someone back there—I saw him do it; he just kind of jerked his head real quick to one side—and then I heard a man whisper, "C'mon, Lucille, damnit, you're makin' a spectacle of yourself." Then, Lucille let a little wail and a long, low moan, and I could hear some scufflin' goin' on behind me, and then Lucille kind of screeched, "Let go me, you son-of-a-bitch! I got a right to be here," and then I heard Mazell Birch say, "Goddamnit, Lucille, get your ass out of this church, now," and then my Daddy said for everyone to hear, "Well, Jesus H. Christ, will someone get that Goddamn bitch outta here!"

After that it was quiet in the back of the church, but I did hear a car make a loud roar and some tires shrill on the blacktop, so I guessed that Lucille had probably left.

It was very nice service for poor Leaky.

Oh, yes. I knew all about poor Leaky and Lucille. Or poor Lucille and Leaky. I don't see how he could of been much of a catch for her, even though God knows he was sweet and kind and gentle and never caused any woman any trouble as long as she didn't want very much from him.

I couldn't never blame her much for fallin' for him. After all, I sure did. He had those big, brown eyes and that look of wonder in them, like he just couldn't figure out where all those little girl babies was comin' from, but I can tell you he knew the answer to that, all right. If he weren't playin' with them babies or workin' he was tryin' to get in as much practice makin' them as he could until he could get it right. I guess that might of been the only thing poor Leaky ever did get right, and he had that down as solid as a cement driveway.

Poor Leaky always looked and acted like he needed a lot of help just gettin' through this life.

He was hard to say "No" to, no matter what it was he wanted, and you always could kind of count on just what it was he wanted.

Anyway, I was kind of relieved when he found Lucille. The only time I ever had any rest was when he sneaked into town to see her, and I suppose I should be grateful to her for that. She never did me any harm, and I always knew he was goin' to come home, cause I knew there wasn't any woman by herself that could handle him for very long at any one time.

Up to when he went out to Mister Sturgis's ranch that day, the only thing he'd ever hunted was a woman. But all of a sudden he had in his mind that if he shot all those little birds, he was goin' to be rich. I tried to tell him he wasn't goin' to get rich killin' any little birds, but I had just as much success tellin' him that as I did tellin' him to be careful when we was in bed alone. Once he got started on somethin', he just couldn't get it stopped.

When I saw Mazell comin' up outta the creek bottom, I didn't have to look at him twice to tell that somethin' wasn't goin' just right. He was puffin' and blowin', and he was white as new laundry.

When no one bothered to say, "Hello," to me, I knew whatever was wrong was wrong with poor Leaky. Just the way they all ignored me and whispered among theirselves, I could tell it had to do with Leaky, and I was pretty sure he hadn't shot all their little birds. I knew it was somethin' about poor Leaky when they come back up and got the horses and went down again, and I had a pretty good idea just about what it was, too, but since they didn't say anythin' to me, I just sat and waited.

I saw them when they came back with Leaky draped over that one horse. That was when I started to think about what I was goin' to do without poor Leaky there to take care of me and the babies. At first, I didn't know what to do. I couldn't drive that contraption, even though I had been the one to give the money for it. My daddy wouldn't of taken to me comin' home just because I ran out of a man. I didn't have any money to speak of, and I sure knew that poor Leaky didn't have any money in his pockets to give to me, either.

I figured that this wasn't so much poor Leaky's fault as it was the fault of Mister Sturgis. After all, if he hadn't of had this hunt, poor Leaky wouldn't of got hisself shot and killed. So it just seemed to me that Mister Sturgis ought to of done somethin' for me and the babies. I thought about gettin' some money to go home on, and then I thought he ought to of donated money to take care of me and the babies.

I just did what I had to do to keep them babies in food and home. I never regretted it for a second, either.

For that matter, I suppose I owe poor Leaky a lot for gettin' hisself killed, too. If he hadn't got hisself killed, Mister Sturgis wouldn't never of put that money in the bank account for my babies to go to school on when they growed up. It was all kind of a relief when he did that, and I guess I got poor Leaky to thank for that.

"Thank you, Leaky," I say every time I think of it.

It's kind of like he made a sacrifice for his family.

The Fragile Commandment

❧

THE HORSE BARN SMELLED PUNGENTLY OF USED LEATHER AND OLD HAY.
The girl had to stand on the tips of her toes to hang the bridle over
the peg. The bridle had to be hung exactly. The reins had to cross
under the bit and then be looped over the peg to hang limply and
hopelessly. There was a reason for hanging the bridle that way, and
she had been told by her mother's husband the reason for doing it this
way. The reins had to hang so that they would remain pliable and not
twist, and the action had become a ritual for her, and she knew that a
deviation from the ritual would have been like breaking a vow.

When she turned Bill was standing in front of her, his legs
braced like thick crossbucks. He stared at her with incandescently
emerald eyes for a moment, and then, before she could raise her
hands, he slapped her with a hand that looked like a gnarl.

She sprawled on the dirt floor. For an instant she couldn't see.
The dirt smelled acrid and old, and then she could feel the heat with
sudden combustion flare over her face, but she thought flaccidly to
herself, "He can't make me cry anymore."

During the unnaturally long seconds she lay in the dust there
was no sound in the horse barn other than her unrestrained and

discontented breathing like the sound of a hairbrush against a floor. She felt as though she was losing her balance on a fence rail and was suspended in a captivated space of time. Then she faintly could hear herself, detachedly, and see darkened forms again and the dread and despair of life came back to her. Finally, her stepfather asked her, "Beth, don't you suppose you could make it back to the house on time? You're nothing but a whore, are you?" he said. "Who were you playing with this time, Beth?" The words flowed like heavy liquid. He sounded to her like he was standing on the other side of the tack room wall in the empty barn by himself.

She had to blink her eyes to focus, to rid her eyes of the tiny, still flickering candlelights. The sound of her breathing was convoluted, like a storm finally foundering.

"Now, hop up, Beth, and go wash your hands and face. You don't want anyone to see you with dust on your face at the dinner table. And tell your mom I'll be along in just a minute, Beth." He sounded as though he were appraising a broken hay rake, apologetic though he had neither responsibility nor any particular interest, since he had nothing to do with its ruining.

She pulled her legs under herself clumsily as though she were only partially awake, and arose as far as her hands and knees, her head hanging to her body and swaying with an unguided restlessness of its own.

When she stood, she was bent like a broken board, and he hit her again, pounding her down into the dirt again, as if her legs suddenly had turned to Timothy-grass, where she lay still at the foot of the pitchfork that rested against the bales of hay. She vaguely heard the sound of his voice, now like a rusty knife, but didn't really hear him tell her that she was nothing but a whore and deserved everything that happened to her because she was filthy. She didn't have to hear each word spoken, since she had heard the litany for two years and had memorized the words the way a person does a ritual without understanding it.

"Nits make lice," he finally said. "Your sister'll be the same way. We'll have to watch her every damn second, or she'll be cavorting around, showing herself for favors and tricks. I'll be damned if I know what makes you the way you are, but you're no damned good, and she won't be, either. I oughta whip her for her own damn good, right now."

She had not cried for a year.

There had been a time when she had not cried at all.

Her now forlorn mother, she remembered, had been like an iris, ethereally fragile, as though even speech might somehow have crippled her. She used to glide like a silver bar of sunlight. She was like a sweet melody that before it became real had been doused in sugar water. Gentleness seemed to emanate from her body in a continual and immeasurable flow. Beth knew that this was because of her stepfather and she had adored him for her mother the way a person is awed by the fragrance of a summer rose. Then, Beth had looked about her with a wonderment and contentment, and when he came to rest, his shirt black with sweat and smelling musky, she sat with him, sipping iced tea. He told her, "No wonder you're so much like you're mother. Just look at all the sugar you put in your tea. You and your mother and little Sally are the three sweetest girls I know."

They would sit on golden chairs at a golden table and listen to the song her mother made beyond them, that faintly lavender and inscrutable strain like willows singing, and she would tell him, "I rode to the West Meadow and fixed the fence just up from the crossing the way you said to," and he would answer her, "I knew I could count on you, Bethy. You saved me a lot of work after supper tonight. You come with me when I milk and swat flies for me, and after we've separated, we'll have fresh cream on that peach cobbler your mommy's fixed."

She and Sally had sat on his great, solid legs that even when he stood watching a stack being built had seemed more permanent than the posts set for the corral. Bucky would hang around his thick neck, and her mother would hum with the sound like a distant bee, watching them laugh under the shade of his arms as though he were a porch, all of them together sounding like gulls circling a bait, and him moaning like a wind-clutched shed, "I can't get up, I can't get up; oh, please let me up so I can go to work." Her mother, her head tilted toward her shoulder like broken flower, smiled at them as they romped over the picnic blanket.

Beth remembered what he had been like before he had hit her, but the remembering had become a vulgarity.

The first time it had happened was after the farrier had left. She had stood next to him and her mother, who continually wore an expression as though the world was an unsolvable mystery and, therefore, inconsequential. The farrier, a thin man with hands like old gloves, had taken a small pink barrette from a metal toolbox and handed it to her and said, "You can have this, Beth. I don't know where it came from, but there isn't any reason for me to have it," his voice like a man dumbfounded over an uncontrollable and natural event, the expression on his face like a man being ridiculed for something undecipherable.

Beth took the barrette and put it in her garnet hair. "Is it pretty?"

"The two of you were made for each other," the farrier said. "Whatd'ya think, Mary Ann?"

Her mother had looked down at her, the barrette like a brilliant firefly settled contentedly in a nest of sunset. "It's pretty," she said, her smile faintly rosy and nostalgic as if she were remembering a young womanhood lost in the dust of a past age. "So pretty," she said again. That night her stepfather had stared at her for some time until his eyes had become like glassy emeralds, and then he had said, "It's the pink barrette that's different," his voice quiet like grain sifting. "Where'd that come from?"

"John McKee gave it to me," she said.

He suddenly and unexpectedly had emanated an intensity like

that a streak of lightning leaves behind before a clap of thunder, and finally he had said, "You come with me." When he led her to her bedroom, without any warning he had slapped her, his hand as rough and stiff as dried and scuffed leather. He yelled at her, the sound of his voice like the sudden sound of a rifle, "You dirty whore! What'd that son-of-a-bitch get for it? What'd you do in the barn with him?" He had jerked her to her feet, smashed his fist into her face, and left her on the floor of her bedroom, numb, as though she had never had any feeling or sense, the metallic taste of blood seeping through her mouth and finally becoming sticky before she could even cry.

She lived like she had been impelled from one essence to another with all her perceptions and cells affected, to exist completely differently than she had before. Every atom of her seemed to have become suddenly aware and brutally conscious, until she felt she might become skinless, except for a continual constriction of her chest and eyes, as though she were being pressed between forces and slowly strangled of her breath. It seemed that the fluids of her body flowed differently, with a sensation of excruciating compression, and in order to relieve this feeling, she tried to withdraw inside her body, to use her thin shield of remaining skin behind which she tried to recoil from a constant strain. She could feel no fluctuation of the sensation at all. There was no ebbing of a tide within her, no feeling of a wellness or a worsening condition, but what had happened to her had become a permanent state of being.

Mary Ann had come to stare at her as she lay on the floor of her bedroom like some old, worn doll with all the firmness long departed from its limbs. She had been flung away like old clothes, making a sound like an old and burdened tree trying to hold back the wind, the laboring of a stricken animal at the edge of its den, and her mother had said to Beth, "You'd better clean yourself," her voice as meager as a flower faded by drought, dry and degenerate. In two years the sound of her voice to her daughter had not changed.

Beth's senses had not been trained to cope with something as inexpressible as what was happening to her. Her consciousness failed to register this for her, try as she might to recall some bit of experience that would serve as evidence for what was beyond her mind's power to encompass. It was like she was without focus, trying to watch wind-blown trees or see individual leaves scatter like frightened animals. She had lost the ability of perception, as though she awoke to find that she had thought of nothing substantial. She felt she possessed the same lucidity as a passing dream, and the alienation of not just her physical body but also of her senses and sensibilities had become complete.

She had stopped crying and screaming a year before because she could no longer stand to hear Sally and Bucky crying and screaming with her.

Lying against the hay bale now, though, she felt at peace and the same moment completely transparent and imbecilic. Her rationality consisted of losing nothing that was happening, understanding everything perfectly clearly; her vacuity was a failure to register even the first stage of any lucid response in herself. There were words going over and over in her mind, words she knew to be dangerous, but words she could no more control than if she heard them spoken by an incoherent lunatic nearby: "You're unable to move." She seemed to not actually exist within her body, but to be so detached as to watch without emotion or interest; to float spatially but nonexistently; she was unharmable, and reasonable precaution did not exist for her.

She pulled herself upward as though climbing a rope, and when she turned, she lunged at him, intently watching the tines of the pitchfork disappear into his throat. It seemed as though he were swallowing the tines without using his mouth. He stood spraddle-legged as like he was waiting to see if he could make time cease to exist and become an eternal man by suspending any and all movement and thought. He had the expression of a man who didn't understand what had happened, and he was waiting for someone to inform him of what was taking place.

When she yanked the tines away from him a tiny spurt of blood shot out of his throat the way a spurt of milk from a squeezed teat might. He made a sound like a boot scraping a rough floor. Then he grabbed his throat, tore at his throat, and emitted a sound like a loose machine, his eyes suddenly full of recognition and inability, his thick legs braced against an animal's attack.

Beth set the pitchfork down in the dirt and she walked away from him. She closed the door between the tack room and the barn behind her and pulled the heavy crossbar over the door. As she walked from the barn she could hear him throw himself against the barricaded door.

The kitchen smelled of wood and bread and milk, greenish and musty. Mary Ann looked like she had never had a transient impulse in her life. She appeared to be no more than a patient penitent, her face overused and now droopy with an utter and probably eternal fatigue. Staring at the flour-smeared counter, she seemed as ineffectual as decomposing cloth.

"Mama," Beth said.

"Beth, you've been a bad girl again. I can see how Bill has had to spank your face. Shouldn't you clean your face?" Her voice seemed to have inherited a permanent dormancy.

"Bill's had an accident, Mama," Beth said, reaching up to remove a wisp of exhausted hair from her mother's forehead.

Mary Ann put her hand to her head as though to hold the thought in place until she was through with it. She stared at Beth with a solemn gravity, a look that on anyone else's face could have passed for a fleeting moment of heroism, but on her face looked like a tinge of idiocy.

"Everything will be all right, Mama. I'll take care of everything," Beth said. She smiled at her mother, a brief and faint smile like the rim of a shell in sand.

Cardinals and Tanagers Flying By

ALREADY THE DAY WAS DRY AS PARCHMENT. THE MOUNTAINS HAD AN iron hue, an oppressed appearance to them, as though they carried a great burden against which it was futile to struggle. Along the creek the willow leaves languished in a light as yellow as old pages, and the water looked like it had given up ever cresting a rock again, making a sound like dry leaves as it flowed listlessly and unarguingly. The day smelled old and faintly bronze.

Earlier the sapphire twilight had been sapless and the kitchen floor felt warm as though there had been a fire that had never dissipated in the night.

Now the kitchen was amber and still.

Wyoma came into the kitchen bringing with her the stale smell of sleep and sat down. The simple wooden chair argued with the floor, and her body hung over the chair like old drapes. Her gray hair was sleek with fresh combing.

When she looked up she had a confused expression. As she stood, she pushed her body away from the table with arms the texture of fish bellies and walked slowly and undeviatingly to a calendar hanging by a ten-penny nail to the sterile wall and with a pencil at the end of a white string marked a line through a day square and said, "There you are, Sir. Thirty-six days, and you haven't rained. You're a very devil, you are." She smiled faintly like a wilting flower. "I know you'll rain. You have to rain sometime, you ol' devil."

Above her she could hear the house telling her that Reece was moving. When he finally came to the kitchen, standing in the doorway like a rain barrel someone had misplaced, the kitchen also smelled of new coffee. Reece settled at the table the way a rock finally halts at the bottom of a hill.

The heat, metallic and powdery, could be smelled as it seeped through the screen door.

"Maybe it would be cool on the ridge under the big fir today. Sometimes there's a wonderful breeze on the ridge, don't you think?" Wyoma said.

Reece looked up at Wyoma quizzically. He had opened his dime-gray eyes as though he meant to see something. When he cleared his throat it was like a gate being closed.

"There isn't going to be any breeze anywhere. Anyway, you know I have to go to town today, Wyoma, honey... after I see if I can squeeze any more water out of that creek for the meadow." His voice had the shrillness of a gull's mew, an inappropriateness for a man as large as he.

"We could go to the ridge and picnic before you go to town," she said. "Yes, we could go to the ridge and sit under the big fir." She smiled, a thin slice of smile as though a remainder of it had to be hoarded.

"I'll just have time to change clothes to get to town and get back for supper," he said. The top of his head looked like a ripening tomato that had contracted a disease.

"We haven't had a picnic for so long," Wyoma sighed. She sounded like a train dying at a station. "If Todd and Mattie come with the children this weekend, we can go then, can't we?" she asked suddenly.

"Yes, by God, and Todd can help me find water for the meadow," Reece said.

When he left the kitchen he looked like an old animal walking upright, Wyoma thought.

The stillness was acute. Wyoma sat at the table with her hand around a cup full of cold coffee. Between her thumb and forefinger she held a cigarette with a long ash, bending curiously and precariously, seeming to defy some physical law, the room once again under a greenish odor not altogether wholesome.

The sunlight was being filtered through an almost opaque window. The light slanted in golden bars as though it had become faintly seared by the heat.

Wyoma's lobelia-blue eyes fluttered momentarily. Suddenly she knew she had not even had a thought, but for how long she couldn't remember. Wyoma, now neat as a newly stuffed doll, glanced at the round alarm clock on the windowsill, and she thought, "Two more hours until the game." Cincinnati and St. Louis. Oh, my poor Cardinals. Cincinnati is going to win the division, I just know it. Damned Reds. It'll be the Reds and the Pirates for the pennant, I just know it. Oh, my poor, poor Cardinals. Oh, what happened to Stan and Enos? And Red. Red won the pennant. Nineteen sixty-seven and nineteen sixty-eight. The series in nineteen sixty-seven. Oh, what happened to my poor, poor Cardinals?

She had set the jar of water on the porch to make tea by the time Reece came back from trying to irrigate. She tried once more to talk him into staying long enough for a picnic. "I can put together a potato salad and some fried chicken in just a minute and we can go to the ridge and sit under the fir. I just know there'll be a breeze there, Reece," she said. Her voice sounded like a saw quivering.

"I gotta go, Wyoma. I can't have George waitin' for me, for Christ's sake. It ain't him that's askin' for money; it's me."

"If Todd and Mattie and the children come this weekend, promise me you'll take the time to have a picnic on the ridge."

"We'll have a picnic, if Todd and his family come. Soon as he helps me get some water into the meadow."

"Little Todd'll want to help you. You can take him, can't you?"

"No reason why not. Time he learned, anyway."

"Not too much longer, and we'll get to have him in the summers, and he can be a big help to you, Reece."

"I'll take him along if he comes, Wyoma, don't worry about it. I'll be back by supper time," he said.

"I know they'll be here," she said.

Wyoma had memorized a little song that she sometimes sang to herself and after Reece had left, she quietly hummed, "Stan Musial had a lifetime batting average of three-thirty-one, hitting over three hundred in sixteen seasons, winning the National League batting championship seven times, named the National League's Most Valuable Player three times, played in twenty-four All-Star games and four World Series. Stan Musial had a lifetime batting average of three-thirty-one, hitting over three hundred in sixteen seasons, winning the National League batting championship seven times, named the National League's Most Valuable Player three times, played in twenty-four All-Star games and four World Series," and when she finished humming, she realized that she hadn't prepared her potato salad for the picnic.

Wyoma counted twenty-four small white potatoes into a pot and filled it with water. She placed the pot on the stove and turned on the gas with hands that looked like kneaded dough. Then she counted out six eggs and carefully placed them in another large pot and repeated the process at the stove. Then she took four pieces of freshly cut and washed chicken, two legs and two thighs, and placed them in a frying pan with two capfuls of vegetable oil and turned the heat to medium.

After she lit another cigarette, she called Rayleen.

"Rayleen, Sweetie, this is Wyoma. How are you?" Wyoma said, her words sounding as though each one had been soaked in syrup and made to sound languid.

"Hot; my God, it's hottern' the hinges a Hell, 'n' I cain't sweat any atall. How are you, Honey?" Rayleen's voice was coarse like scuffed leather.

"Oh, I'm excited. Todd and Mattie and the children will be here this weekend. I'm planning a big picnic."

"Oh, that's wonderful. My, I'll bet those grandchildren have grown. My God, it's hot. How can you stand it? Burl hasn't been able to irrigate the meadow for five days. The hay's burnin' up."

"Reece can't get any more water out of the creek, it's so low. He doesn't know what we're going to do. The hay's so short and scraggly, Rayleen."

"It's just terrible. It's lasted so long. Burl says he cain't think of a time when it's lasted this long."

"I haven't seen my tanagers for so long. Oh, how I miss Mister Tanager's bright flashing by my porch," she lamented.

"It's the heat, Honey. They've all gone somewhere for water. They'll come back when there's water, Honey. Don't you worry none."

"I do worry about my tanagers, though. What if they've died?"

"They've just gone away for a while, Honey."

"Well, I just had to tell you about Todd and Mattie and the children, Rayleen. I'm going to listen to my baseball game. You take care, now."

"Oh, you, too, Wyoma. Bye, bye."

"Goodbye."

The only sound in the kitchen was the water boiling in the pot. It was as though any sound that might have entered the kitchen through the screen door had been stifled by the heat before it could reach the porch. When she heard the sound of the boiling water, Wyoma looked at the alarm clock. The game would start in an hour. She remembered that on May second in nineteen fifty-four Stan Musial had hit five homeruns in a doubleheader. Then she hummed her song again.

She still didn't like the divisions. She couldn't get used to the

Dodgers not being the Brooklyn Dodgers. She wanted the Cardinals to play the Brooklyn Dodgers, not the Los Angeles Dodgers, and sometimes when that team from Los Angeles was playing, she wouldn't listen to the game because they really didn't exist. And the Atlanta Braves were not really a part of the National League, nor were any of the other new teams, and as far as she was concerned they wouldn't ever be, not really. They were just upstarts that shouldn't be allowed to play against the real teams that had men like Stan Musial and Enos Slaughter and Red Schoendienst. The San Francisco Giants. It was disgusting. Why couldn't they have always been the New York Giants? Oh, they couldn't ever do anything like that to her Cardinals, could they? They could if you didn't watch them. If you didn't watch them, they would do it some winter when there was a storm and she couldn't do anything about it.

Maybe someone has taken away my tanagers. Maybe I won't ever see Mr. Tanager again, she thought.

Suddenly she felt overburdened as if there had been another child to bury.

She peeled the potatoes and shelled the eggs as though they were live coals. She cut each of the small white potatoes into twenty-four neat pieces so that they appeared to have been born from the same litter, and then she cut each egg into twenty-four pieces and placed them in a bowl with the potatoes.

Stan hit four hundred seventy-five homeruns and collected three thousand six hundred thirty hits.

She mixed in a bowl twelve ounces of mayonnaise, two table-spoons of mustard, two teaspoons of dill pickle juice, and one-quarter cup of canned milk and stirred diligently until the mixture looked like thick lemon juice. She poured the mixture over the potatoes and eggs, stirred everything for four minutes, and covered it with a cloth dish towel.

She turned the pieces of chicken, which by now were the color of softly tanned leather, and turned the heat to low.

In nineteen forty-two Enos had collected one hundred eighty-eight hits.

She placed the chicken on a white china dish that had tiny roses and lavender leaves wrapped around its edges and covered it too with a cloth dish towel. In a wicker basket, in the bottom of which was a folded red and white checked tablecloth, she carefully placed two red plastic dishes and two peach-colored plastic cups, and then she put in two neatly rolled yellow linen napkins into which had been wrapped silverware. She placed the plate of chicken in the basket.

When she walked outside with the wicker basket, she felt as though she were drying up, as though her skin suddenly had tightened across her face and had squeezed every bit of water from her.

The inside of the pickup was hot, and the seat was like freshly branded hide. Even by the time she had returned to the house and then carried the potato salad, sun tea, and the radio to the pickup, the inside of the cab had not changed. When she touched the steering wheel she jerked her hand away and squealed. She had the sudden thought that she might not be able to drive to the ridge and the tree. Her mouth was like a taut clothesline. Then, the next time she touched the steering wheel, she knew that she would be able to drive to the ridge and the tree, and her mouth turned upward so that it finally looked like an open window.

The ridge looked like the back of an animal and the fir looked like an old man who, if he ever walked again, would need a cane. The tree looked comforting.

Everywhere she looked the land was dry and pintoed with alkali. When she looked across the land it seemed like a giant antelope pelt.

The day was as still as an old leaf and it smelled metallic and irritated the tongue.

Later, there was music on the radio and the potato salad was bright yellow. Wyoma was hunched over the tablecloth. "Oh, I've missed the game," Wyoma said. Her voice sounded discordant like an untuned piano. Then she looked across the tablecloth and used a smile that had been dipped in sugar water, and she said, "Oh, well. We have had fun, haven't we, Stan?"

"Yes, we certainly have, Wyoma. As usual your fried chicken was delicious," he said, smiling, his face smooth. He picked up his bat and stood lithely, as though he might have been weightless, smiling down gently at Wyoma, seeming to pamper her. "We've got the Giants next, Wyoma, wish me luck. I have to go now."

"Oh, yes, now that the game is over, I have to go. I have to be back and have supper ready when Reece comes. You know our hay isn't going to be any good, don't you? Of course you do, you ol' devil."

Everything smelled still.

Someone's Dog

DICK HAD NO IDEA HOW LONG THE DOG HAD BEEN FOLLOWING HIM, but he suspected it had been moving through the brush with him for some time. He had been intent on his fishing, and suddenly the dog had been there. It had startled him.

The morning came slowly up the canyon, bringing with it a high, blue ribbon of sky, a white, brittle sun, and a breeze that was neither warm nor cold but was made up of late winter or early spring, depending upon how one chose to think about it. It was a fragile day, one that could slip either way.

Female rainbow trout, egg-heavy, were moving slowly upriver, close to the shoreline or very deep near the rocky bottom of the river, avoiding the faster, thicker currents of the North Fork. They were moving toward the small, very clear tributary streams, up which they finally would run to spawn and then either die of exhaustion or drift back down into the North Fork for another year before they again would heed what Dick labeled "the mysterious call to propagate their species."

It was for these trout that Dick had driven up the canyon, as he did every year at this time, his first effort to thrust his way past winter. He always opened his season by fly-fishing this spawning run, every year to be amazed again at the strength of the rainbows' instinct, the beauty of their spawning colors, and the power in their lithe bodies during the short, furious battles against him.

The first place fished was at a bend of the river. A long and swift riffle lived between two large, sheer-sided points of granite. After the riffle, which could be fished only in periods of very low water, was the blue pool that brushed against the steep outside bank of the bend. On the inside bend of the pool was a rocky bottom that was easy to see in the river before runoff. The water was so deep on the outside bend that the bottom could not be seen at any time.

Dick waited, with the constant sound of the riffle and an occasional, intimate sigh of the breeze as it caressed the pines, until the morning turned the granite points pink and the pines green but still left a great shadow over the river. Then he crossed at the tail of the pool where the water was shallow and he walked up to the inside bend where the current eddied and where the rainbows paused to gather strength for the narrow, white-topped riffles between the granite outcrops.

He cast his large black-and-white Bitch Creek Nymph to the little choppy waves between the current and the eddy, and allowed the big nymph to sink to and drift its way over the rocky bottom.

There was no strike in the usual sense. There was just a slight drag on the green fly line to tell Dick that a rainbow had mouthed his nymph, and he set against the trout with a quick lift of his rod tip. The fish turned away from him and moved downstream with the current, and he let it move almost freely, barely coaxing it away from the current, moving it subtly into the shallower water where he could see it, all the time holding his arms high above his head, feeling the trout's fight in his shoulders. He watched the trout lunge against the leader he couldn't see, and then the rainbow turned back toward the current. He brought it back by making no offer of slack line. The argument between the trout and the rod tip was short, and he walked quickly toward the fish, reeling as he walked to keep tension between himself and the trout, faltering on rocks, his concentration completely with the fish, stepping high in the water to miss the tops of the rocks, but once stumbling, which brought a quick "Goddamn!" from him.

Dick brought the trout to him. She was deep-bodied, her belly swollen with eggs, and her sides were silver. He knelt next to her, and without touching her he felt his way to the nymph and with a quick twist took the hook from her jaw. She didn't move. He stayed with her while she held herself steady in the shallow, cold water, gaining back her strength to continue her spawning run that had been so abruptly interrupted.

"C'mon, gal. You're okay. Just rest a minute; no one'll hurt you," Dick told her as soothingly as he could, as though she would hear and understand him. Her tail shimmered for a second, and she sped through the rocks away from him, leaving a wake behind her. In a moment she had disappeared. Dick didn't move. He sat quietly and watched the current to see if she would slowly glide to the surface, spent and dying. He always tried to play spawners quickly and release them gently so they could continue their mission. Finally he rose, knowing she was safe.

He caught and released another heavy female before he left the pool on the bend. In the next two hours he caught and let go four more rainbows, three females and one vividly black-spotted, orange-striped male that weighed at least three pounds. By then the breeze was gusty and becoming cold. The willows, which did not have buds on them yet, waved like rod tips when the wind, coming like a drum roll, swept among them. When Dick walked through them, they lashed at him.

Between casts, he watched the sky for signs of snow and sometimes he paused to smell the air, but the canyon walls hid most of the sky and the air smelled only like the pines that covered the canyon in tiers.

He stopped on a rock bar between the willows and the river to cast to a stretch of swift water that was scourging the far bank, carving an undercut. When he turned his head to see where the willows were for his backcast, he saw the dog and it startled him.

The dog was lying at the edge of the willows, his forelegs extended and crossed in front of him, his hind legs drawn up under him. His eyes were gray and his face was like a black butterfly, each of his gray eyes set in a black triangle that would have been the wings of the butterfly. The same black stretched over his back and tail. It occurred to Dick that he was being examined by the dog, although perhaps the dog was only staring back at him. Finally made to feel nervous by the animal's gaze he said, "Hello, Dog."

The dog did not acknowledge him. Dick then considered that the dog might be waiting for a command of some kind, but Dick did not offer the dog any satisfaction. The dog was not his and he had learned growing up that if a dog did not belong to you, you did not speak to it unless to give it a command. The dogs he had known had been working dogs. They had belonged to ranchers, and the rancher he had worked for all those years ago had been very explicit concerning the accepted behavior toward working dogs.

"You're not bein' mean to 'em, Dick. You're helpin' 'em, doin' 'em a favor. Keeps 'em from bein' whipped. You git friendly with a dog that ain't yours, and then the owner has to go an' whip the dog to git him back to minding him. So, remember that you're helpin' the dog by not speaking to him," Mose had said. He had repeated that admonition more than once, and the concept had been ingrained into Dick, so that forty years later it did not occur to him to question it.

"If it ain't yours, don't do anything to try to make it yours," Mose had said, and Dick had heard him, although sometimes he wondered if he had not heard Mose too well, because there had been many times when others had thought him to be unfeeling toward dogs, if not outright hostile to them.

It was true that Dick did not have a great love for dogs, but he did not dislike them, either. There had been two dogs in his child-hood that he had loved. Tucky had belonged to his grandparents. Tucky was a black and white dog that he barely remembered, and if pinned down to recall just where the black had been and where the white had been, he would not have been able to do it. But he did remember the feeling. Whenever the thought of Tucky visited him, it always came with a distant choke, along with memories of his grandparents and his mother and a far-away time that could not be captured again. The second dog had been Nipper, his small black cocker spaniel, and when he remembered Nipper he had to look away because of the intense memory of how he cried knowing that when Nipper had died, she died alone and she would have wondered where he was and why he wasn't there. The shame of not having been with her then had made him hide, and the crying had come in gulping sobs that had shaken his body. He had not had a pet since then.

There were definite things about some dogs that Dick did not like. He did not like dogs that continually fawned and groveled, and as far as he could see, most of them did. He did not like dogs to shed on him. He did not like dogs that dug holes in yards, particularly his, and he did not care for the smell of a wet dog. But he did not dislike dogs.

"I'm going to cast, now but I'll be careful of the backcast. If you just stay right there, you'll be all right," Dick said.

The dog neither moved nor made a sound so Dick turned to the river and cast. He had three good drifts, but nothing happened, and he turned and moved slowly downriver, stepping carefully in his clumsy wading shoes over the rocks along the bank.

A cold wind came and Dick could feel it against his back, and he thought he should have had sense enough to pack a sweater into his fishing vest. He remembered the dog, and he turned briefly to see the animal following at a respectful distance in the manner of some-one bored with the proceedings. Dick continued downriver, thinking it would hurt nothing if the dog followed him for a way. It was obvious that the dog was well trained and cared for. The dog either had been left along the river on purpose, or he had been forgotten. Dick did not think the dog was a runaway, because whoever had the dog had cared for him very well, and dogs do not run away from kindness and care. The possibilities, however, confused Dick, because he could not understand the circumstances under which anyone would abandon such a beautiful dog, nor could he understand how anyone could forget about such a dog and leave him.

He stopped and turned around. The dog stopped and looked at him.

"You're not going to tell me, are you?"

The dog did not respond in any way, so Dick turned back to the river. He stopped suddenly and turned and looked upriver. The piece of blue sky above the canyon had been swallowed by gray cotton, and now Dick could see and smell the snow. He looked down at the dog, and without any hesitation he said, "I have to go now," and he walked away. He did not look back, even after he reached his Ranger.

Monday through Friday, Dick always met Paul and Bill for ten o'clock morning coffee at the Country Kitchen.

"I found a dog yesterday," Dick said. "Actually, he found me."

"Where?" Paul asked.

"North Fork."

"What kind?" asked Bill.

"Maybe a husky. At least a northern dog."

"Husky, malamute, or Eskimo?" Bill asked.

"I don't know. It just looked the way a husky should look."

"Tell me," Bill said.

"White, gray, and black. I don't know. His face had a black blotch like a butterfly, at least that's the way it looked to me. His back was black, not all black but with a wide black streak, and his tail had the same black on it. I don't know what else to tell you."

"Could have been any of the three," Bill said. "They look alike, unless you know them pretty well. The Siberian husky, Alaskan malamute and Eskimo are all pure breeds, though."

"What'd you do with him?" Paul asked.

"Left him."

"Any idea what he was doing there?"

"No. Strange, though. Beautiful dog. Great shape. Very well trained. He just sat behind me and watched me fish and followed me for a while. I just don't see how anyone could lose a dog like that. Don't see how anyone could just run off and leave him, either."

"It's someone's dog," Paul said.

"How does that kind of dog get along out here?" Dick asked Bill.

"A lot better than others," Bill answered.

"Will he eat fish?" Dick asked him.

"Sure. I've had three of them that were crazy about fish. Kusko was the craziest. He used to sit right next to me and as soon as I got a strike, he'd leap up and charge into the water after it. You ever try to land a seventy-five-pound husky on a 5x leader? He'd chase the fish all over the pool. It didn't make it any easier trying to catch another fish in that pool, either."

"Some really like fish, then?"

"Raw and whole," Bill answered. "One gulp."

"He should do all right, then?" Dick asked.

"Yes. Too bad he's lost or something, though."

Dick could not stop himself from thinking about the dog, particularly in the evenings when he was tying flies or reading or putting together subdivision specifications. The dog invaded his mind, and it made Dick so uncomfortable he had to get up from his desk and find something else to do. But the dog always came back to him and watched him pace through the house. Sometimes in his mind Dick would let himself call to the dog, and the dog would come to him, and he would reach out and touch it, and they would go fishing together. And when he let that happen, he could hear Mose saying, "It's not your dog. Leave him be."

But he wanted to see the dog again. He wanted that very much.

Friday morning Bill asked him, "You going to go up the North Fork tomorrow?"

"Yes," he answered. He had known all week he was going to go back up the North Fork, and he knew he was going to look for the dog. He knew it would not hurt a thing to just see the dog to be sure it was all right.

"Going to check and see how the dog's getting along?" Paul asked.

"Yes," Dick answered.

The dog found him. He was fishing the hole above where he had left the dog the previous weekend. He had been fishing for an hour, sometimes glancing behind him, sometimes standing very still and searching the gray, barren willows and the green pine stands for shadow movement that would betray the dog's presence. But there had been no shadows moving. The morning was clear and cold, and around the rocks at the shore's edge there were fringes of clear ice. There was no breeze, and the only sound was that of the river on its way to Cody. He just turned and there was the dog.

Dick had not realized how tense he had been with expectation until he saw the dog, and then his chest seemed to drain and slouch and his shoulders to sag.

"I've been looking for you. How've you been doing?" he asked.

The dog returned Dick's look for a moment before looking away with what might have passed for indifference in a human. Dick continued to look at the dog until he realized just how beautiful the dog was, and he suddenly was very surprised at just how much he had been seeking the dog, wanting so very much to see the dog again. It was like finding a lost good friend from a long time ago.

Then a shadow moved through him, and his chest muscles contracted, and he tightened all over again and he felt as though he just been caught stealing candy and a lot of people had seen him do it. He turned back to the river and cast. "Let's see what happens," he said.

He caught a twelve-inch cutbow, and after he slipped the gold

Ribbed Hare's Ear from its jaw, he grasped it and turned to the dog and tossed it to him. The dog lunged at the flopping silver cutbow and caught it, pinned it between his front paws, and it disappeared into his mouth, and after what Dick judged to be two quick chews, the action was over and the dog settled again into his prone waiting position, his gray eyes glancing at Dick and then away.

"Not hungry, are you?" Dick asked, and again he felt the sag of his body and he found that he was smiling.

The dog glanced at him, but neither moved nor made a sound. Dick took his time to look carefully at the dog. Its coat had sheen and gloss to it, and although Dick knew very well that the dog was tense, waiting for him to repeat the fishing maneuver, the dog had a natural ease about him. Perhaps a natural command of himself, Dick considered. Bill apparently had been correct that a dog like this was perfectly capable of taking care of himself.

"You're not too bad, Dog. I could learn to like you," Dick told him.

❧

They fished together that day. Dick worked the riffles and small pockets where he thought the smaller fish might be, and he caught eleven more cutbows, all of them between twelve and fourteen inches. He tossed four of them to the dog, who waited patiently and took them as quickly and decisively as he had the first one.

Dick felt an exhilaration as the week of expectation drained from him. He slipped easily into enjoying the dog's companionship and his role as provider. There was a joy in sharing his activity with the patient dog.

The day became not a thing just happening, but a thing that always had been between him and the dog, a feeling of the familiar, of knowing. For Dick the day—the present—had both a past and a future to bind all life together. It was a moment new and already mature and wise, and the only one of its kind ever created. It was then that he decided he would allow the person who had lost the dog another week to claim him. After that he would take the dog. It would be time to do so. He knew it.

Finally, the time came when Dick knew he was going to leave, and he steeled himself to going away from the dog. He purposely broke the spell that had bound the two of them that day as they had raced through the afternoon together. Only when he reached his Ranger and sat behind the steering wheel did he relent, and then he turned and said to the following dog, "I'll be back next weekend," and then he left.

"Did you see the dog?" Bill asked.

"Yes. He looked good. Had a good time with him. Damn, does he like fish! A chomp and it's gone," Dick told them, smiling and feeling good with the memory. "We walked along the river and fished quite a bit together before I left."

"Did you leave him?" asked Paul.

"Yes. He's not my dog."

"He's been there a week," Paul said.

"Have you heard anything about a lost dog?" Bill asked.

"No," Dick said. "I've been reading the *Gazette* and the *Tribune* every day to see if someone's looking for him, but there hasn't been anything. Nothing in the *Enterprise*, either."

"Why didn't you bring him home with you?" Paul asked.

"Not my dog," Dick said again.

"Look, Dick, he's been there at least a week. If you don't take him, someone else will," Paul said.

"Why would I want him?"

"You do," Bill said. "It shows in your face when you talk about him."

"I don't know."

"What are you going to do?" Bill asked.

Dick didn't reply right away, but he knew his answer. Finally he said. "Maybe if he's there this weekend, I'll see if he wants to come along. Would there be anything wrong with that?"

"No," Bill said.

Dick had a week to think about it. Now, when he thought about the dog, he allowed the dog to come into his house and lie before the fireplace while he worked at his desk, and Dick talked to him, telling him about his work, and then the two of them would discuss where they would go fishing next. The dog did not ever answer Dick, but sometimes he would leave his cozy place before the fire and sit next to Dick, and then Dick would see again how beautiful and powerful the dog really was. He would want to reach out and touch the dog, feel the beauty and power and warmth.

Then suddenly, he would realize what he was allowing himself to do, and he would stand and shake away the thoughts because he knew he shouldn't think that way about someone's dog, and then he would become afraid of the dream, afraid of the coming weekend and afraid that nothing would be the way he dreamed it to be.

He read the newspapers and waited.

Saturday morning as Dick drove up, the North Fork was clear, and although the blue ribbon of sky rested on the tops of the cliffs, there were shadows in the canyon and because of the dark shadows the little, brilliant silver clouds hanging from the ribbon were too bright to look at for very long. The gray buds were at last turning into green things on the willow stems, and Dick knew that if the weather held just a few more days the waters of the North Fork would be brown like coffee with cream, and the rocky bars where he and the dog had been standing and fishing the past two weeks would be covered with swirling, ugly water.

He drove to the pool where the dog found him and he fished there for an hour, drifting a Gold Ribbed Hare's Ear and then a small, black Woolly Worm with a brown hackle. At the end of the hour he had caught three small cutbows and a rainbow, a small male that was still bright with its spawning colors, and each time he brought one to his net, he looked into the brush for the dog, but the dog had not come.

He fished down the river, spending less time at each pool, thinking more of the dog than of the fishing, until the time he spent looking for the dog was more than the time he spent fishing. But all he found were some dog tracks, large ones like those of the dog, but they were not fresh by at least two days. Finally he quit fishing and devoted his whole time to looking. At first he felt weak, as though he were going to faint or be sick, but as he continued to walk through the willows and into the pine stands along the river, listening, hearing only the chatter of an early Steller's jay, he regained his composure. By the time he left the North Fork canyon late that evening, he again knew he had no right to someone's dog, and what he had dreamed was not a dream he could have.

"Well?" Bill asked when he sat down.

"Wasn't there," Dick said.

"Too bad."

"Not really. I don't know what I would have done with him."

"Gone fishing with him," Bill said.

Dick did go fishing with him. The dog rode in the cab of the Ranger and they went fishing together. He lay in front of the fireplace, his front paws crossed and his head resting on his paws. He crossed the floor to where Dick sat reading and lay at his feet. The dog was a good dog, and Dick loved the dog. The dog didn't fawn over him, or whine, or shed or smell the way wet dogs smelled. The dog came when Dick wanted it to, and it left when Dick's mind drifted away. The dog was such a good dog, and Dick did not ever worry that he might lose him.

Yesterday...

The Great Mormon Cricket
Fly-Fishing Festival

❧

PROBLEMS ARE RELATIVE. FOR INSTANCE, WHEN DAVE AND JACK
borrowed Wat's new red and black Ford Ranger to go antelope
hunting, Wat felt the possibility of a problem arising, but he loaned
it to them anyway. He did it because they were friends. He also did
it because his new pickup was in far better condition than Dave's
poor old gray International, and he knew that if the International
died of old age while crossing the desert, he would have to go after
them, wherever they might be. So loaning them his pickup seemed
the easier thing in the long run. He also knew they would bring him
enough antelope meat so he could make his sausage, the secret recipe
of which he was ready to defend with his axe. He particularly liked
antelope sausage and two eggs over easy for breakfast.

And he also did it because it was his responsibility. He was not
born with this responsibility, nor had he sought it; he was given it by
Dave and Jack years before, because they knew that Wat seemed to

think things out better than either of them, and also because allowing Wat to take care of them gave them time to utilize their energies in other positive ways, none of which Wat had ever been able to find although he had searched for years. Wat had considered the possibility of a problem.

Still the loan of Wat's pickup had solved a problem for Dave and Jack, a problem significantly larger than any tremor Wat might have had over loaning his pickup truck. Like Wat, Dave and Jack had considered the possibility of Dave's International not coming back from the hunt, but being left to bleach forever in deep sand. And there was much more to their worries than that. The International probably would have failed before they could get their antelope. This, in turn, would have meant they would have to return from their hunt empty-handed, and that would have meant a lifetime of derision from Fanbelt to Mule Creek Junction. Along with being laughed at for having been so foolish as to take the International more than five miles from the nearest service station, not getting their antelope, and then, on top of all that, having to be saved, well, it was just too much for them to look forward to. Had they been subjected to all they imagined, they would have been duty-bound for a weeklong drunk, and they could not afford such a luxury. Wat had solved their problem for them. Their relief had been great. It had been a close thing.

It was not until Wat's pickup sank to its hubs in a sandy draw that either of them suspected that something they had not planned was happening to them. The four-wheel drive could not take them out of the sand. But it did manage to push them deeper into the sand. Jack tried to push. Finally he said, "Damnit to hell, Dave! Get your ass out of that truck and help!"

"Who's going to drive it if I have to push it?"

"Figure it out for yourself."

Challenged, Dave considered it. This was no small chore. It was not that he was incapable of thinking; he had just not put in a lot of practice doing it. It was like building a haystack: if you haven't done it for a long time, it might not look right.

Dave walked along the top of the draw and found a long stick, a branch that was old and white and brittle, the final one from a colony of willows that had long since vanished in the turquoise wilderness. Carefully, he measured the distance from the accelerator to the steering column. He cut the stick to the measurement. He started the Ranger and placed the stick against the accelerator and wedged the other end under the steering column. While the Ranger churned in the sand, he ran to the rear of the pickup and both he and Jack leaned into it, their feet sinking into the sand the way horses' hooves sink in the mud. The Ranger moved slowly out of the sand and up the slope of the draw. But when Dave and Jack fell gasping in the sagebrush, the Ranger kept going slowly. It moved in a very wide circle and kept moving in wider circles for three hours before it ran out of gas seven miles from the sandy draw.

When Dave and Jack finally caught up with the Ranger and rested until their breathing and body temperatures reached almost normal and the sweat stopped burning their eyes, they filled the tank with gas from a spare can Wat had placed in the bed, just in case, and an hour later they got their antelope. They did not mention to Wat their having to use the spare gas and Wat had the good sense not to ask about it or about why they were limping. Consequently, there had been no problem to rend the fabric of life at Fanbelt. Maintaining appearances is important in successfully avoiding problems. But there came a time when a particular problem could not be avoided by merely maintaining appearances. On this occasion, the sport involved was fishing rather than hunting, and the problem was not vehicular.

The proportion to which a problem may rise is predicated upon the intricacy of the prelude to the action. This is a well-known adage that came into use following the Fanbelt Fly-Fishing Club's Great Mormon Cricket Festival, although there still are many people in the state who are not aware of it or the festival.

Fanbelt is a crossroad between Douglas and Gillette on a north-south highway, although Fanbelt is not what the crossroad has always been called. An east-west road crosses here, but it is not a highway. It is a dirt road that unravels around hills, swoops without warning into dry washes filled with rocks that tear mufflers off pickups, and then forges on through miles of hazy blue sagebrush and grass country. In the summer, the highway is very hot and the sagebrush country through which it cuts is very dry. Only at Fanbelt are there any trees or water for fifty miles in any direction. Sometimes in winter the highway cannot be driven at all because of the wind-blown snowdrifts that cover the country, and when that happens Fanbelt is alone.

Fanbelt once was a tepee, and then a hog ranch and then a store and finally a gas station. When Wat bought the old building, he made it into a truck stop. He built a restaurant and bar and garage, and Fanbelt once again became an oasis, a diamond surrounded by emeralds in a turquoise ocean.

One might not think that a fly-fishing club would grow at Fanbelt, since the only water there is barely enough to wet the sand under the cottonwoods in the spring. But Corky thought Fanbelt could have a fly-fishing club, and so, with Wat's assistance and the use of the bar as a clubhouse, the idea grew rapidly. At one time, there were seventeen members of the club. They met the second Tuesday night of every month, unless, of course, there was a blizzard or it was haying season. The club flourished, even though there were some Tuesdays when only Wat, Corky, Dave, Jack, and Ross were on hand to carry through the club's business.

There was a series of omens not seen as such that could have foretold the coming problem, but at the time no one thought about them. Being aware of omens is very important in problem recognition. Only by utilizing omens can a problem reach its proper proportion in relation to reality. The first thing that happened was that Dave discovered the club didn't have any money. He wanted the club to buy him a drink for having remembered to bring a pad and pencil to take minutes of the meeting, but within moments Corky discovered that the club did not have a treasury in which to have any money. Wat pointed out that the club didn't need any money, because the club didn't ever do anything but come to his bar and mooch drinks. No one gave it any further thought until two months later, when Corky innocently said, "I ran into Duff Barton the other day when I was in Casper and he said the Casper Fly Casters were going on an outing to Miracle Mile and they had enough money in their treasury to invite us. He said they were going to have hamburgers and beer. We don't ever do anything like that."

"That's what I tried to tell you," Wat said.

"Why don't we?" Jack asked.

"Because all you want to do is come here and tie flies and mooch drinks, and whenever we go fishing we all go together just like we have ever since we were kids," Wat said.

"We ought to do something," Dave said, sitting up, his head rising out of his shirt like a turtle's head from its shell.

"It'll cost money," Wat said, trying to defuse what he recognized as a situation that in all likelihood was going to cost him a lot of cash.

"How do we get money?" Ross asked. Ross had selective hearing. Even though he usually answered a question with "Huh?" there were key words that brought him to an intense state of awareness, words such as "money," "trout," or "woman" usually being enough to bring Ross into any conversation.

"You collect dues from club members," Wat said.

"What?" asked Dave.

"You collect money from club members. You collect dues. That's how clubs get money," Wat said.

"There ought to be another way," Jack said.

At the next meeting, Corky said, "I talked to Duff Barton and he said their club has moneymaking activities."

"Like what?" asked Ross.

"You know. Bake sales and raffles and auctions and stuff," Corky said.

"I can't bake," Dave said.

"Even if you could, no one would eat it," Jack said.

"Why don't you go to hell."

"All right, that's enough," Wat said, seeing the possibility of a broken pool cue looming over the room. "If you want a treasury, you have to elect a treasurer, and if you want money in the treasury, you have to make some money to put into it. What do you want?"

"I sure as hell don't want Jack to be the treasurer," Dave said.

"By God, you can go straight to hell," Jack said.

"Stop it, damnit," Wat said. "We have to have a nomination for the office. Who do you want? And I'll be damned if I'm going to do it for you."

"Hell, let Corky do it," Ross said. "It's mostly his idea, anyway."

"Yeah, it was Corky's idea," said Dave.

Corky was elected treasurer by acclamation.

"Now what about raising money?" Wat asked.

The topic was tabled until the following month. It was within that month that one of the mystical happenings of the world took place, but that event was not recognized for what it was. The Mormon crickets migrated.

A real migration does not usually occur every year, although there certainly are Mormon crickets on the move at some place some time. Their minor activity may not be noticed, but a real migration of Mormon crickets is easy to recognize. The ground for miles in any direction appears to be waving, and just above the ground will be hundreds of birds. Cars have been known to slide off highways because of the cricket goo created by the tires crushing thousands of them. There only is one cricket more ugly than the Mormon cricket, and that is the Jerusalem cricket, which is so ugly that after new-comers to California see a picture of them, they no longer will go barefoot in the grass at night.

The Mormon cricket actually is a shield-backed grasshopper, a katydid. In the summer, the female lays her eggs in the ground, and the following spring the young hatch. By summer, they are full-grown and ready to devour anything in their path. It was the Mormon cricket that almost sent the Mormons back to Illinois from the Great Salt Lake valley in 1848 when a swarm descended upon their fields. Fortunately, the gulls came and ate the crickets, and the Mormons were able to keep their fields. The saving of the Mormons by the gulls is commemorated yearly in Salt Lake City. Birds are the only things on earth that profit from the Mormon cricket. That fact did not alter Corky's enthusiasm one bit when his idea came to him in a flash of inspiration.

⤚✦⤙

Thoughts come to people in different ways. For instance, when Dave and Ross thought of asking Wat for the loan of his Ranger, the idea had come to them only after several days of contemplating their problem. They had tried other solutions, such as fixing the International, which would have entailed both work and money; they had thought of walking, but that they also discarded because they would have blistered their feet walking in their cowboy boots and, anyway, the rifles were heavy enough without having to carry back an antelope; they had considered asking to go with someone, but that kind of dependence they recognized was demeaning to hunters of their reputation. They only thought of borrowing Wat's pickup because it was sitting in front of them during one of their contemplations. The pickup had loomed out of the fog before them, and they had almost run into it before they had recognized it.

Corky's inspiration on the other hand came to him in a flash with trombones and reds and silvers and golds and the cheers of crowds. It marched past his eyes like a band in a parade.

"We're gonna hold a festival," he said.

"A what?" Dave asked.

"A festival. We're gonna invite all the clubs all over the state to the festival, and we're gonna have hamburgers and beer and we're gonna raffle off a couple of fishing rods and we're gonna invite the governor to speak and we're gonna have a band and we're gonna have a fly-tying contest and then we're gonna all go fishin'."

"What the hell are you talking about?" Wat asked.

It was all very clear in Corky's mind. The next spring, when the Mormon crickets came, the Fanbelt Fly-Fishing Club was going to have a Great Mormon Cricket Fly-Fishing Festival. Corky's mind was not always clear to others, though.

"Where the hell we gonna go fishing?" Wat asked.

"The ranch reservoir. It's been three years since the Game and Fish stocked it after that big winter kill there, and those brood-mare rainbows have got to be ready by next spring. They'll be huge. You know how fast they grow in that reservoir. We'll offer a prize for the biggest fish."

"If we're gonna be offering all these damn prizes, how we gonna make any money?" Dave asked.

"Simple," Corky smiled. "You gotta pay to take part!"

"What if no one wants to take part?" Jack asked.

"You telling me all those guys won't want to enter a fly-tying contest and a fishing contest? C'mon. They'll pay anything if we make it sound big enough. We'll make this the club championship of the state. We'll be rich."

"Rich" is an interesting word, a relative word. What is rich to one person may not be rich to another. However, if one is broke, such philosophical hairsplitting usually does not enter into the discussion. To Dave, "rich" meant a chest full of golden doubloons, sparkling diamonds, rubies, emeralds, pearls, and lustrous silver goblets. To Jack, it meant a Texas fifth of Seagram's VO. To Wat, it meant trouble.

"Oh, my god!" said Wat.

Corky called Al Lindner at the Game and Fish office to make sure about the crickets.

"Well, Corky, it's hard to say. There're always a few crickets around, but a big migration like we had this past spring doesn't happen every year in the same place. There may be a few that will be out, but I sure wouldn't count on another big migration for a while."

"We can commemorate the Mormon crickets even if they don't show up," Corky told the club members at the next meeting.

"Oh, my God!" Wat said.

Corky visited the shops in Sheridan and Buffalo and Casper, and actually was promised four fly rods as donations: two Sage rods, an Orvis rod, and a Loomis rod. Although the governor had to decline the invitation to speak on June 23, the day of the festival, the state water engineer volunteered to speak, which made no sense to Wat since there wasn't any water at Fanbelt except what came out of the sky or the well. Mr. Wilson, the Midwest High School band instructor, volunteered the members of the band for the festival; the women of the Light of God Church auxiliary of Douglas volunteered to bake pies, cookies, cakes, and candy for a split with the club. They also volunteered to help in the truck stop if Wat would volunteer it, and Wat volunteered his truck stop with its kitchen and bar for the festival.

"But you're gonna have to pay for the hamburgers and booze and beer. I am not going to give that to the club!"

"We'll have to owe you. After the festival, we'll have the money."

"Oh, my God!"

⚬≋⚬

Letters were carefully written to all the fly-fishing clubs in the state explaining the festival and inviting all club members to tie an imitation of a Mormon cricket to enter in the fly-tying contest—the winner of which would receive a 3-weight Loomis mahogany blank with matching wraps, and a reel seat with black-anodized sliding rings over the cork. Each club member taking part in the festival would have to pay $2, and Corky thought the club might take in close to $700. After paying Wat for the hamburgers and beer and picking up any other expenses, they might come away from the festival with maybe $100, which would be enough for one hell of a fishing party to Outlaw Canyon for the five of them after the winter runoff was over. Maybe they would even extend an invitation to one of the other clubs if there was anymore money left over.

By the second week of February, Corky reported to the club that there probably would be around three hundred fly-fishermen at Fanbelt on June 23.

"You've done a fine job, Corky," Wat said.

"I did a lot of networking," Corky said.

"A lot of what?" asked Dave.

"Networking," Corky answered.

"What the hell is that and how much did that cost us?" Dave asked.

"It's what they do in Casper, and it didn't cost anyone anything, damnit. Don't you know anything?"

"Don't get smart with me, Corky. What's networking?"

"Talking."

"Oh."

"Why didn't you say so?" asked Jack.

"I did."

"Open up the bar and let's network a while, Wat."

"Hell, let's go to Lusk and network at Millie's," Dave laughed, slapping the bar top.

"All of you go to hell!" Corky yelled.

The ice melted off the ranch reservoir in mid-April after one of the coldest winters anyone could remember, and a week later there were four- and five- and six-pound rainbows floating and rotting in the water. No one could recall such a winter kill before. Even the one three winters before wasn't this bad. This winter had been a disaster because when the ice came, the reservoirs had been low for lack of rain during the preceding fall. The thick ice destroyed fishing a lot of places that winter.

By the first of June, it was obvious to University of Wyoming extension agent Harry DeVore that there would be no Mormon cricket migration this year because of the weather conditions.

On graduation day at Midwest High School, a three-quarter-ton silver and blue Chevy pickup, driven by Oscar Wheelan, backed over the band's instruments. On the fifteenth of June, the entire women's auxiliary came down with an intestinal virus, and on the twentieth the state water engineer's secretary called to say that he would have to cancel his speaking engagement because he had to attend a water conference in Billings.

All of a sudden, worries were circling Corky's head like buzzards. Corky had a problem. Dave told him about it.

"Well that's just great, Corky! What're we gonna do now? This was all your idea. Damn if we aren't gonna look like fools, Corky. If you hadn't wanted to get rich, this wouldn't have happened. You really blew it!"

"You and your damn networking," said Jack.

"Maybe you oughta go live in Casper," said Ross.

Not only was the Great Mormon Cricket Fly-Fishing Festival in jeopardy, but Corky had let his friends down, and, finally, self-doubt seeped into his head and began to whisper things like: "You thought you were so smart! You thought you could handle the whole thing. You really blew it, Corky! You couldn't do it and you let your friends down. You're a jerk!" Corky sought dark places. No one had ever had a problem like this before.

Just as there are omens to be read concerning the coming of disaster, so are there signs that point to fortune's entrance. Wat was the first to discover fortune's footprint. It happened early in the morning, two days before the festival was to begin. Wat was sitting at the counter, sipping a cup of freshly made coffee, when he found that he was watching something slowly crawl across the glass pie counter. He focused like a microscope on the crawling thing. It was one of the ugliest things he had ever seen. "Damnit to hell! There're crickets in my restaurant!"

There were a lot of crickets in his restaurant. They were in his bar and in the garage too, and in his bedroom behind the bar. Gobs of them. More than anyone had seen in one place before. There were at least a hundred of them in the drawer with the spoons.

It was as if the coming of the crickets was the signal for which fortune had been waiting. By midmorning, the women of the auxiliary had recovered. By noon, the insurance company had sent a check to the school to pay for the destroyed instruments. And in a stroke of unprecedented good luck, no politician could be found to replace the water commissioner.

"All I can figure out," said Harry, "is that the conditions were just perfect for them hatching under your garage, Wat. Not too cold, not too hot, not too wet, not too dry. Just right."

"Well, what the hell am I gonna do to get rid of 'em?"

"Nothing. They'll be gone in a couple of days."

"I can't do business with a restaurant full of crickets and birds, Harry."

"Nope. Probably can't, Wat. See you."

When it was over, Wat calculated that the days' loss of business and the cleanup had cost him $2,500.

But good things came out of the cricket infestation. The festival was a great success, even though everything and everyone had to move to Lake DeSmet for the bake sale and hamburger dinner and fishing contest, and, of course, Corky, who had begun to lose weight with worry, was a hero. Since that time he has been considered a prophet in the land.

The following year, six hundred fishermen came to Fanbelt for the festival, so great had its renown become, and the year after that there were over eight hundred who came to take part. Wat reckoned that he actually had made up the money he had lost the first year.

Corky even saw him smile just a day after the festival ended that third year. What had appeared to be an insurmountable problem turned out to be a mere bump on the trail. No matter how hard Corky and Wat had tried to make a problem out of the festival, they just couldn't do it. Sometimes problems can be very disappointing.

Bonefish in Wyoming

CLINT WAS IN HIS THIRD DAY OF WAITING FOR THE STORM TO SPEND ITSELF.

A short man with white hair and keen blue eyes, Clint's face was creased with gullies from spending his life squinting into the sun, and although he moved slowly he moved very well for having ridden more horses than he should have. Few people guessed he was as old as he was. He was wearing new Wrangler blue denims and neatly polished brown cowboy boots. His shirt was white with pearl snaps, and his suspenders were bright red.

He sat in the Towne Hotel bar watching through the side door as the rain cascaded over the old, worn-out building. The Towne Hotel was muggy, the white-painted stucco falling away from the bricks of the outside walls. The paint on the inside was new, but the hotel was one of those places that would look tired no matter what one might do to it. There were trees with bright red blossoms along the sidewalk, and the street appeared to be vibrantly alive. There were houses along the street that were pink and green and blue, and farther up near the top of the hill where the huge, pink Governor's Palace squatted, trees grew purple and blue flowers. Across from the hotel was a large white church, neat and clean, and sometimes its bells tolled peacefully over the city. But not much of anything was going to help the Towne Hotel.

The rain came in sudden bursts. There would be a few minutes of stillness and then a few minutes of torrent and wind, and the roar was so great no one could hear another person talk.

Clint was not feeling good. The total weight of feeling that one has is always the same. Feeling flows through a person the way mercury runs from one side of a saucer to another when the saucer is tilted. Sometimes there is more feeling on a good side, and sometimes there is more feeling on a bad side, but the amount does not change. A person is born with just a certain amount of feeling. When a person begins a fishing trip, most of the feeling is on the good side, and it will stay there if a person catches fish. But if a person doesn't catch any fish, the feeling spills to the bad side. Very seldom is the feeling evenly distributed. Clint's feeling was flowing heavily to the bad side, and he was beginning to think the storm might not end and he would not get to go fishing. He had just three more days before he had to leave.

"The bonefish is a ghost," the man sitting across from him said. He said it very quietly, just as he said everything.

"What do you mean, 'ghost,' Richard?" Clint asked. He tried for two days to have a conversation with Richard, who had been pointed out to him his first day at the Towne as a man who knew a great deal about bonefishing. Richard owned a fishing resort on Andros Island. He was waiting for the storm to end, too.

"He has a changeable color, and sometimes he's there, and sometimes he's not there," Richard said, "he comes into the shallows and mangrove swamps where he feeds on crabs and shrimp and snails. He comes in with the tide, and he follows it into the swamps. When the tide goes out, he follows it into the flats," Richard said, speaking very carefully to make sure Clint was following him.

Above them a gold-bladed fan lazily stirred the humid air, and

Norma, who was large and neat, stirred drinks behind the bar, mostly the Bahama Mama, the tourists' favorite rum drink, and emptied large, white, shell-shaped ashtrays. Every once in a while a native conversation would rend the stillness between the convulsions of the storm. Sometimes there would be more than one native conversation from one end of the bar to the other, but no matter how many there were, they all seemed to be able to cross the room in midair without colliding with one another. All the native conversations were very loud and very rapid.

Clint found that two English languages were spoken by the natives. There was one meant for the tourists to understand, and another meant for the tourists not to understand. Whichever one was spoken, it was spoken very quickly and very loudly.

Richard's hair was gray at his temples. Whether or not the rest of his hair was gray Clint couldn't say, because he had never seen him without his blue cap. Richard was wearing a blue, Bahamian short-sleeved shirt with white palm trees printed all over it. Most of the natives Clint had seen, if they were not wearing suits, wore T-shirts. Clint found that if he wanted to see Richard smile he had to watch his brown eyes where his smile nested. When Richard spoke to Clint, he always spoke very softly in the Bahamian English meant for tourists to understand.

Clint listened closely, even though much of what Richard had been telling him he already had read in books before he came here to go fly-fishing for the bonefish. He had spent months reading everything he could find, even going back to an old book by Joe Brooks, trying not to miss anything and wanting to be ready. He had read so much that he was able to see and feel how it was going to be when the bonefish made its run after a strike. That is the thing about the imagination. The imagination will not show a person a bad cast or a missed strike. The imagination always shows the imaginer's best cast and the best strike and the perfect set against the strike. The imagination always shows the greatest fight from the best fish. The more a person knows about something, the better the imagination can make things. Imagination is everyone's bulwark against final disappointment.

By listening to Richard talk softly about bonefish, Clint's imagination kept working, and so the wonderful feeling of anticipating a fishing trip was still inside of him, even though the good feeling was beginning to slip across his saucer to the bad side due to the wait. It was hard to wait out a storm by lying on a bed and staring at a ceiling, even if there was a fan on the ceiling that slowly turned and stirred the air just a little. It was easier to wait it out in the Towne Hotel bar drinking Bahama Mamas. When Clint had someone to talk to, it was even easier, especially if the person talked about fly-fishing for bonefish.

"You will have to come to Andros with me and let me take you fishing," Richard said.

"I'm going to, but I have to leave in four days. I have just three days left to fish. Will the storm be over in time?" Clint knew it wouldn't be over in time. He could smell the storm and the smell was strong.

"I don't know," Richard said, looking away from Clint, "but let me tell you what we'll do. When I take you to them, I will choose a fish that is on the side of the school, because that one is ready to leave the school, and casting for that one will lessen the chances of spooking the whole school." Everything Richard said sounded confidential as though it were meant only for the person he was talking to. It was nice to be talked to that way.

"I will edge you in very quietly to about thirty feet from the target I have chosen for you. I will point you at twelve o'clock to you quarry. Do you understand twelve o'clock?"

"Yes. I know what you're saying."

"Good. If I do that, then you will know exactly which one you are going to cast to. Then, I will turn the boat so you are at ten o'clock so you can cast, and the reason I will do this is because I don't want your fly in the back of my head." He smiled at Clint, but Clint knew that he wasn't kidding about having a fly in the back of his head. Clint smiled back and said, "I understand perfectly."

"I will give you one false cast to make, and then you will have to lay your fly three feet in front of the fish," Richard said, sipping his gin and milk. "Too many false casts can spook the whole school," he said, looking into Clint's eyes.

"I understand."

"When the fly hits the water, your rod tip will be at nine o'clock. Instantly drop your rod and take a short strip." Richard used his arms and hands to show Clint what he meant. "Follow the short strip with a long pull, and then lift your rod tip. That is when he will hit your fly."

"I really want to go," Clint said.

"When the storm is over, we'll go to Andros."

"If it ever ends."

"When there is change in the weather, the ghost can be fussy, and the rest of the time, he is just unpredictable," Richard said, and Clint picked up the smile in Richard's eyes.

Two hours later, Norma told him he couldn't have anymore Bahama Mamas because there wasn't anymore coconut rum, so he ate a dinner of conch from the buffet and then went to bed. Before he went to sleep he watched the fan for a long time and he imagined the strike of the bonefish and felt its tremendous run. The wind and the rain and the fan finally put him to sleep.

The next morning when he went outside the street was littered with torn green palm fronds and shattered red flowers. The street looked as though it finally had given up trying to hold up everything and had suddenly let everything fall on it. There was broken glass of many colors on the street and sidewalk, along with wet gray papers and bent green palm fronds sticking out of the mud.

But the sky was blue, the air was heavy with the smell of the salty ocean, and the white church looked as clean as ever.

Clint was dressed in white pants and shoes. For a month before he left, he had practiced walking in the shoes, pacing back and forth in the bunkhouse, so they wouldn't hurt his feet when he wore them in Nassau. He was wearing a light blue shirt, and he had on a tan straw hat with the brim turned down in front. He had bought the pants, shoes, shirt, and hat especially for this trip, because he had an idea that people dressed that way where it always was warm, and he knew that he was one of the best looking tourists in Nassau. Only if you looked at his face and hands could you tell that he worked hard outdoors.

He walked toward the harbor, hearing the pigeons and wondering if people made towns where there were pigeons or if the pigeons came to the town after the people built it. He had not ever lived in a town, but every town he knew had pigeons in it.

He had learned to listen to the Nassau traffic. If a car horn sounded, he knew it was time to jump for the curb because everyone drove fast and no one stopped for walkers. They only warned them.

There were rollers on the ocean, and when they hit the breakwater on the far side of the harbor, great spumes of white shot high into the air with a continuous dull roar. It was the harbor that Clint had come to see, and when he saw it his whole body knew there would not be any trip to Andros or any fly-fishing for bonefish for at least two days. Knowing that, he walked to the pier and took a small boat to the other side of the harbor to Paradise Island, where the small boats were moored and there was a large, beautiful hotel with a casino. It was the small boats that interested Clint.

He had prepared himself for this morning. He had read about the dolphinfish and their furious attack, and the wahoo and their swift strike, and the more than five hundred species of groupers in this ocean. He had known for some time that he would have to make a change, but he felt that if a person didn't say something bad aloud, there always was a chance that the bad thing would not happen. It was only when a person said aloud the bad thing that it would happen, so he had not said aloud that he was going to have to give up fly-fishing for the bonefish. It was just superstition, of course, but sometimes, he thought, it really worked, at least he thought he remembered that sometimes it had worked. But last night he knew he was going to have to make a change.

He could not go back to the bunkhouse in Wyoming and tell everyone he had not gone fishing. They all had given him a small leaving party, and his nephew, Ray, who owned the ranch—the ranch Clint's brother, Chris, had owned, the ranch that he and Chris had started and built, the ranch he had worked for and lived on all his life—had given him a little extra money for this trip. He would have to have something to tell them.

"Ay, mon! You want to go fishing?"

Clint saw a smiling young man standing on the stern of a white fishing boat. The black lettering told him it was the *Key Runner*.

"Yes," he answered.

"I get the captain," the young man said and disappeared below. In a moment another man came topside. The man was dressed in a blue flannel shirt, cotton denims, and brown leather loafers. He had long brown hair that was very curly, a mustache, sideburns, and blue eyes. He was tall and slim.

"You want to go fishing?"

"Yes."

"Tomorrow. Too rough today. The next day would be better."

"I have to leave then."

"We'll go tomorrow. Two hundred dollars for a half-day. Where are you staying?"

"The Towne."

"I'll pick you up behind the Sheraton on their pier. Seven o'clock in the morning."

"I'll see you then," Clint said. "What's your name?"

"Captain Reggie Orange."

"I'm Clint Baker."

"O'kay, Boss. Tomorrow."

"You want any money now?"

"Tomorrow."

"Tomorrow."

Satisfied with his work and finally feeling good again, Clint walked back over the harbor bridge to the main island. He skirted the conch vendors, who shouted, "Ay, mon come see my conch! I sell them pretty cheap to you! I got good ones, mon! You can take them home with you!" He walked all the way back to the center of Nassau. He had lunch at the 18 Parliament Street Restaurant on the outdoor veranda. He had a hamburger and a bottle of Beck's. The Beck's tasted so good he left right after eating because he knew if he had another one and it tasted that good he might want to stay and have several more. He still had a long way to walk back to the Towne, and he could smell more rain coming.

He felt so good he went by the Straw Market, and after wandering through the isles of native goods for a long time, he finally let a large woman sell him a straw hat that had "NASSAU" sewn on it with violet lettering. After he did that, he spent the rest of the walk back to the Towne trying to think of what he would do with the hat. By the time he reached the front steps of the hotel, he had decided to give it to Ray's wife, Dolores, and she could put it in the closet for the rest of its life.

His feet hurt.

That evening, still wearing his white pants and blue shirt but now wearing his brown cowboy boots, Clint walked down the hill to the large hotel on the harbor front to have dinner. Afterward he stayed to drink a Bahama Mama in the bar with the rest of the tourists. Now he felt good. He was going to go fishing, and the old feeling, *It's going to happen, and it's going to be fun!* was back with him.

They sailed out of Nassau in the morning aboard the sportfisherman *Conch*, which had been tied next to the *Key Runner* the day before. The *Conch* also was white. The tall tuna tower made it look top-heavy. The sky was dull silver and the wind smelled like the ocean. Beyond the harbor, they could see waves pounding the breakwater, and beyond that they could see swells rolling like blue hills being moved one over the other.

Captain Orange from the flying bridge guided the *Conch* toward the gap in the breakwater and toward the open water. Clint sat quietly watching everything. Below on deck Derrick, the young man who the day before had hollered at Clint, rigged rods and baited the lines. By the time they slipped through the breakwater, they could feel the cool breeze, and when they reached the open water, it was too hard to walk on the deck because of the wind and the swells, so Clint stayed with Captain Orange until they cleared the reef. Then Clint went down the ladder to the deck and sat in the fighting chair.

Captain Orange came parallel with the reef, and Derrick slipped the fishing lines over the side. They were fishing with downriggers.

"We're fishing for wahoos, kingfish, and dolphin, Sir," said Captain Orange. "We're fishing right along the shelf now. If it was summer, we'd head right out to sea, maybe ten or twelve miles, but this time of year we'll stay close to the island."

Clint nodded and kept watching the rods and lines. Anticipation filled him, his every sense was keyed to the fishing and to the ocean that arched and swayed and dipped around him. They were things he had not ever seen before, and he watched intently. Watching had been his whole life, and learning by watching had meant life. What was happening to him now was new, and when, for the first time, he saw a flying fish break the surface and glide away, skimming over the waves to finally disappear into the ocean, he looked up at Derrick and smiled and said, "First one I've seen."

"You will see many more, Mister." Derrick smiled back.

For an hour Clint watched and waited, and then Derrick said, "If you want to go up with the captain, it's all right. I will call you if something happens."

Clint climbed up the ladder and sat down next to Captain

Orange, who turned toward him for a moment and said, "I have been at sea since I was fifteen, and a captain since I was eighteen. I have been all over the Bahamas. What is Wyoming like?"

"Mountains and plains and deserts," Clint said. "The mountains have snow on them, and during the winters we have snow everywhere, sometimes as high on the level as this bridge."

"I wouldn't like that."

"You'd like the summer. In the mountains it's nice and cool, and there's plenty of trout to fish for."

"Mountains. I don't know mountains."

"They're pretty nice. Where's the *Key Runner*?"

"Ah, she's at home. She's larger and we don't need her today. I'm going to change the name of the *Conch* to the *Key Runner the Second* to go with my other boat. I've had this one six months, and I've had the *Key Runner* for three years."

From the bridge, Clint watched Derrick bait the hooks again, this time with a small silver fish on a lure with an orange head and chartreuse feathers. "What are we doing now?" he asked Captain Orange.

"We are staying between one hundred fifty and one hundred eighty feet. This is where fish will congregate to feed on smaller fish. Most of the time, wahoo and kingfish travel in pairs, but sometimes they travel in larger groups. In the summer at sea we'd look for flocks of gulls feeding near a school of bonita or dolphin," he said.

They trolled for a long time. The day did not become any lighter, and the water was gray. Only if Clint looked down alongside the boat was the water blue.

Sometimes he saw other boats. Some of them were charter sportfishers like the *Conch* and sometimes he saw very large sailboats—one of them had two masts. The sailboats belonged to people who lived along the Atlantic Coast and spent the season sailing from the United States to the Bahamas. He watched them until they disappeared behind a swell, and then he would try to guess when and where they would come back into view. They always came back, but not always when he guessed they would. The game helped kill time.

Captain Orange took his binoculars and scanned the constantly shifting ocean, and when he put the binoculars down he came to port and put the island astern. He radioed another boat called the *Miss Tiggy*, and when the other voice came through the fizz, he said, "I'm going to sea to look for dolphin. There's nothing here."

He turned to Clint and said, "We're going to look for kelp beds, or any kind of drift, because the dolphin will feed on the small fish that follow drifting things."

He left the radio on, and every once in a while there would be distant chatter about how the fishing wasn't any good that day. They listened to the chatter for some time, and it always was the same about no one catching any fish, but neither Captain Orange nor Clint said anything about the chatter.

After a long time, Captain Orange said, "January and February are good out of Nassau. It should be good now. Today is just a bad day, Sir."

Clint nodded and stood up and climbed down the ladder to the deck. The boat was rolling badly on the swells. Derrick pointed to the cabin, and Clint went inside and sat down in a chair. There were two chairs, a sofa, and a small table that could be unfolded to make a big table. There was a small icebox and a sign that read, "Free beer tomorrow." It was a neat cabin. On another day it probably would have been very comfortable, but the boat was rolling too much to be able to sit in the chair peacefully. Clint went back out on deck and sat in the fighting chair to see if that would bring luck.

He sat for a long time in the fighting chair, but nothing happened, and finally he knew that nothing was going to happen. It was a bad day, Sir.

After another quiet time of sitting and waiting, he heard a soft whistle above him, and Derrick began to reel in the lines.

"I didn't catch you any fish, Boss," Captain Orange said from the bridge.

"It's no great tragedy. There have been other times when I didn't catch any fish."

"When do you leave Nassau?"

"Tomorrow."

"Will you come back again?"

"Yes."

"We'll go again."

"And catch fish."

"And catch fish," Captain Orange answered, but both of them knew Clint was lying about coming back. Their voices gave the lie away. They didn't talk anymore until Clint left the boat, and then he turned and said, "If you ever travel to the United States, come to Wyoming. Remember my name and just ask for me."

"I'll remember," he said, and both of them knew he wouldn't do either thing.

Clint drove into the ranch very late at night, smelling the coming weather, but when he came in everyone got up to see him, and they wanted to know how the fishing had been and if he had caught a bonefish.

"I didn't get to go bonefishing because of the storm." Clint told them and then he said, "I went out trolling one day with a guy, but we didn't catch anything. But I did bring a recipe and the ingredients for one hell of a drink, though, and come Saturday night I'm going to mix a batch of it."

He waited until the next day to unpack after everyone had left the pine-log, one-room bunkhouse. Then he took the white pants and white shoes and light blue, short-sleeved Bahama shirt and tan straw hat and neatly repacked them in a cardboard box. He carried the cardboard box up to the storage area over the room and left it there among the other cardboard boxes, many of them covered in dust. Then he unpacked two bottles of rum and a bottle of Nassau Royale and put them in his olive-drab World War II footlocker.

Finally, he sat down in an old stick rocking chair. Its wood seat was covered with a dilapidated maroon pad molded by years to comfort, and he leaned back and closed his eyes.

He was warm, and he saw a very clear, very flat stretch of blue water. He saw the bonefish and he raised his fly rod quickly and after one false cast he sent the line after the bonefish, and he gave the line a short strip and started a long pull when the bonefish struck the white fly.

He opened his eyes and looked through the window. Small, white flakes of snow were drifting past. He closed his eyes again and his reel whirred as the bonefish ran, strong and hard. Later, he thought he heard Richard softly say, "He's a ghost."